# When Double Becomes Single

by

## Charmaine Gordon

Vanilla Heart Publishing

**When Double Becomes Single**
by Charmaine Gordon

Copyright 2015 Charmaine Gordon

Published by: Vanilla Heart Publishing
www.VanillaHeartPublishing.com

This book is a work of fiction. Names, characters, places, and incidents are either the product of the author's imagination or are used fictitiously, and any resemblance to places, events, or persons living or dead is purely coincidental.

ISBN-13: 978-069250-72-16 ISBN-10: 0692507213

10 9 8 7 6 5 4 3 2 1 First Edition

First Printing, August 2015
Printed in the United States of America

# When Double Becomes Single

by

Charmaine Gordon

# Table of Contents

Dedication and Acknowledgements

More Great Books by Charmaine Gordon
Charmaine Gordon Author Bio and Photo

# Dedication

I dedicate When Double Becomes Single to all the widows and widowers who find themselves alone for the first time. I've been there and know it's a struggle to begin again. Making a new life requires courage and strength. I learned to face each day with a smile; take one step at a time and somehow time passes. You can build a life and find happiness the second time around.

# Acknowledgements

Because you believed in me, I believed in me and so we became a team. Thank you, Kimberlee Williams, for being a wonderful friend and the best publisher ever.

Thanks to Weekend Writing Warriors, an online blog that cheered me on every step of the way as I wrote *When Double Becomes Single*.

Reviews are important to writers. When you read any of my books, please take a moment to review. I'd so appreciate your kindness.

# Chapter 1

The touch of her husband's lips on hers warmed Sharon Michaels all the way home from the hospital. Remembering his whispered 'I love you' before she left released a cascade of tears. She groped in her bag for a tissue, found none and used the sleeve of her good winter coat as a blotter. Mac would fix Barry. Their favorite doctor always knew the magical potion to apply. Even when Fred, their difficult teenager now in his thirties, started using marijuana and refused to stop, Mac knew what to do. Tough Love was the prescription. No driver's license or other privileges allowed until he straightened out. So Barry's bad cough should be easy, like the croup. Hmm. Fred still held a grudge against us. Get home and go to sleep.

Exhausted after hours visiting with her husband at Community Hospital in Suffern, New York, Sharon stripped and pulled on flannel pajamas. Too tired to shower, she brushed her teeth, washed her face and slipped under the comforter on this chilly night. The phone rang. She picked it up. Mac Bloom, the family doctor said something she couldn't quite hear.

"Crisis? Is that what you said? What do you mean crisis? I left him at the hospital about an hour ago. We kissed and said I love you the way we've always done for thirty-six years."

Their doctor for many a long time sighed. She heard urgency and sadness in his voice. "Sharon, is anyone at home with you?"

She laughed and heard a touch of hysteria rise in her voice. "Of course not. Barry's in the hospital with a bad cold and cough. You make it go away, okay?"

"Please, Sharon, listen to me. Can you drive here or should I call a cab for you right now?"

"Oh, Mac, now you sound serious."

"I am. Come now." He ended the call.


In a daze, she dressed, headed downstairs, pushed the garage door button, and wondered vaguely if there was enough gas in the tank. Soon she reached the highway, paid the toll and sped west to the hospital as ordered. She blinked over and over again. The trip from their home in the suburbs at midnight with a light snow falling reminded Sharon she'd forgotten her glasses. Where was the snow shovel and who would do the job of cleaning off the driveway and the long walkway? It was too soon for her since hip surgery still had healing to go. A lot of mending had to happen in this thin body. Barry always called her his pocket wife, so small he could tuck her in his winter jacket.


She parked, then stumbled toward the hospital entrance in her hurry to the third floor. The empty elevator suited her, a ghost town so late at night, dim lit and quiet. Something triggered an impulse to RUN.

Down the hall she ran toward Barry's room, hip throbbing, where outside in the hall Doctor Mac Bloom paced. He stopped her from rushing in.

"Sharon, he's had a heart attack. A bad one. There was nothing we could do to save him."

She shook her head. Snow captured in her blond hair fell to the floor. "What do you mean, Mac? You always fix everything. You're the one..." She grabbed his white coat. "You're saying Barry's gone? He's dead?"

One big shove at Room 304 and she flew past the doctor and in to where her husband lay still, his hazel eyes closed, gone forever from her life.

"Get out, get out," she shouted at the nurse who wiped at Barry's mouth with a cloth. The nurse left. His checkered robe hung in the open closet, slippers tucked below, forlorn and shabby without Barry. His toothbrush showed blue toothpaste she'd seen an hour before. Sharon used the step stool to climb up on the bed. She needed to be closer, to touch and caress his face. Already he felt cool to her lips.

"Barry, come back to me. You just left. Don't leave so fast. There's still time to return." She wrapped her slender arms around his big frame but the longer she held her husband, the cooler he felt. She shivered with grief. "God, take me instead. My husband's the brains of the outfit. He's the leader. I follow." Her fists clenched knowing it's too late, too late.

The doctor entered the room. "Sharon, it's time to say goodbye. Go home. Call your sons. I know one lives out of town, New Jersey, I think, and the other lives...where?"

Tears flowed. "He lives in Denmark, far away. Barry will be cremated. I'll save the ashes for our younger son, Jeff. They were so close." She met his eyes. "Death is harsh."

With that, Sharon left to wonder how she'd ever survive without him.

15

# Chapter 2

1:30 a.m. in New York 7:30 a.m. Denmark

Skype

"Mom, what's up? You never call this early." Jeff, the youngest son, squinted at the screen to see his mother crying. "Oh God, Mom. It's Dad. Last time we talked you said he had a bad cold. He's gone, right?"

He watched her cry without stop, heartbroken to know his dearest Dad died. Through tears, Mom told the whole story. Inge, his beautiful wife, came running from somewhere in their house. They held each other as they listened to the worst news. Jeff's father dead and they're so far from his home in the states. Jeff felt a crack in his heart where solidity had always been.

"We'll catch the next plane out, Mom. They are lenient with a death in the family. I'll get back to you."

"But your dance school, who will take care of it?"

"Don't worry. We have the best dancer who takes charge when I'm not here to supervise. Inge wants to talk to you."

"Mamse, what a terrible loss. Jeff will pull strings to get us to you as fast as possible. Try to get some rest and know we love you and we'll be with you soon."

"Inge, talk to me. You and Jeff are my lifeline right now."

"Mamse, when I was but a young girl, my father died and left us with nothing, so my mamse had to work in a shop mending clothes for rich people. She didn't want me to be an artist later on but art was in my blood, as you say. It was a calling I listened to and before long, my work was looked upon with favor here in Denmark. I became well known and one day, a dance team came here to perform and there he was, our Jeff. I fell for him right away, like a groupie, and followed him a few times in countries nearby. So now we are married with our precious babies, your grandchildren. Here is what I wish for you to do, Mamse. You, one day, sell your home and move here where we have lots of room for your privacy and before the children are too big getting. Did I say it all right?"

"Perfect. Thank you, Inge. You've helped though a few bad minutes. I'll see you tomorrow. Have a safe journey." She closed the laptop, severing the connection.

Jeff rushed in. "We have tickets. We'll be home by evening tomorrow." He stopped short. "Oh. You and mom are finished."

"Yes." Inge wiped tears from her fair skin. "She is so helpless right now. Your father did everything for her and she followed. It's better the way we are, more independent." She ran long fingers through his graying hair. "I love you, my Jeffrey. How special that we first met in Copenhagen when you were performing."

"Love at first sight, sweetheart." He caressed her back to soothe both of them. "Mom's going to have a tough time. Can you imagine Dad always at the wheel of the car? How will she ever become independent?"

"Oh, she will. I know in my heart she will."

Skype. What a wonderful invention. So many times she and Barry talked to the kids since they moved to the far way country to begin a business. And how successful they'd become. Jeffrey Michaels School of the Dance became the place to learn dance artistry. With all his training in the states and dancing throughout the world, Jeff had a great reputation. When he and Inge met, the lovely Dane so gifted in the art community and the American dancer, they became a match. Too bad she and Barry had made the long trip to Denmark just once for the wedding and another time to see the babies.

She needed a glass of Chardonnay before calling her older son, or maybe two glasses to fortify the distance between them. New Jersey was close, but they weren't, and for some reason never had been, and that wife of his always grated on her nerves. Sharon found an open bottle in the fridge, poured a glass and sipped. Again the pajamas went on, and once again, she washed her face, patted it dry, and smoothed on a bit of cream so she wouldn't dry out.

Finally, liquid courage helped her punch in his number... 3 a.m. in Asbury Park, New Jersey. Corrine picked up. Sharon heard shouting in the background. How charming. Just what a mother loves to hear.

"Yeah? Who's calling?"

"I'm sorry to call so late, Corrine." Don't cry, don't cry. "May I speak with Fred?"

"Oh sure. Freddie, it's your mother."

"Mother, what's wrong? Oh God, Something must be very bad for you to call this late."

She took a deep breath to calm herself. "Fred, your father had a bad cough and a fever. Doctor Bloom suggested he stay in the hospital and, and... " Another deep breath, "He had a heart attack and just a little while ago he died."

Silence on the line. "Can you just shut up for a minute, Corinne. My father had a heart attack and now he's gone."

Sharon heard more mumbling in the background before Fred got back to her. All she wanted to do was go to sleep. Where did her son ever learn to treat a wife without respect and love? The boys grew up in a peaceful loving home.

"Is my brother coming in from wherever the fuck he lives?"

"Of course, and don't curse."

"So you called him first, huh?"

"Stop it right now. I have no patience for your rivalry. He needs time to make arrangements. It's a very long journey from Denmark. Now I'm going to bed. I need rest before the," her voice caught on the word before she could say, "funeral."

"We'll come up tomorrow to help with arrangements. Goodnight, Mother. I'm so sad to hear this terrible news." Sharon heard her oldest son break down as he hung up the phone.


Sharon didn't want help. She didn't need anything from her son and that wife of his. She rolled over to Barry's side of the bed. Whimpering came from the area of Barry's closet. She lifted her tired head. There stood the two rescue dogs saved to live with them a few years ago. The sweet pit bull Tommy moved close to his best pal Gracie, a chocolate Lab Setter. They were always sensitive to what went on in the house and when Barry began coughing, the dogs climbed on the couch, one on each side of him as if to protect him. Sharon patted the bed to allow them to climb up for comfort. She knew Barry didn't care anymore.

# Chapter 3

Early the next morning, Jeff called. "Mom, we'll be landing at La Guardia this evening. A driver will bring us home to you. Did you get any sleep last night?"

"Thanks to Gracie and Tommy, I did all right. Your dad wouldn't mind they slept with me and I wore his robe. All the good smells I'm used to are in the robe. Oh, Jeff, how will I survive losing him?"

"Move to Denmark and live with us. Inge and I talked about it. We have lots of room and the kids would love you to pieces like we do."

"Denmark? Thanks, honey but there's the business. Dad and I built a reputation for so many years." Sharon reached for a tissue to catch another flood of tears.

"One more thing before I have to hang up. Listen carefully and consider my advice. Even though I'm the younger son, I've made a success in business and marriage. I'm sorry to say Fred, on the other hand, is not to be trusted. His business is in bankruptcy."

Shocked, she didn't know what to say. "How do you know? Isn't that private?"

"There are ways to find information. You and Dad have a successful business with a reputation for quality service. You've furnished exceptional cabinets and counters for years. Fred will take advantage saying he wants to help. Maybe he'll bring in that wife of his. He knows nothing about business and he'll rob you, I just feel it. I'm sorry to pile this on you right now but we're private at this minute and we must get back home in a couple of days. Just one more thing, my mom, you will be getting a substantial insurance check from Howard, your old pal. Hang on to it, protect and invest it with a company. We'll see you later. Inge sends her love."


Sharon held her head as the coffee brewed. She knew their sons had issues with each other but Jeff never expressed himself this way about his brother. "Barry, did you know about the enmity between our sons?" Her heart raced just thinking about it. Parents have children thinking how sweet... little companions. Does it ever work out? She'd have to figure this out for herself.

As she tended to the dogs needs and made coffee and toast, Sharon made a plan, her first attempt on her own.


"George Ferguson, this is Sharon Michaels. I need your services today."

The somber voice spoke in low tones. "Mrs. Michaels, whatever you need, we are at your call. We know your dear husband passed on last night. Please come here and make arrangements. If you prefer, I'll send a car for you."

"Thank you. That's very kind. I will be ready at ten."

"Mrs. Michaels, my sincere condolences. You and Barry were very generous when we remodeled our kitchen."

OMG, this is hard. Consider it step number one. Next step is take care of dogs and figure out what to wear. Black or gray.

After showering, Sharon did her hair and picked out a gray silk dress, one of Barry's favorites. And what for him? She dabbed at tears so willing to flow as she went to his closet filled with casual clothes and suits. Barry loved his velour warm ups, especially the dark blue set. And what to take on his journey, she wondered. Sharon had a box of pictures to look through, discarding single shots and selecting doubles so she could keep one of each. Baby pics, marriage pictures, and so many happy memories. Finally, with make-up on, she still had time to make a list of unpleasant things on her mind right now.

In the office, she booted up the computer for privacy and typed.

1. Fred and Corinne don't like our dogs.

2. They can't be trusted.

3. They will try to take advantage of me.

4. Insurance money, where to invest it.

It's a start, she thought, and entered the slim document into a private file.


The Ferguson Funeral Home driver arrived. Sharon locked the door and hurried out, the small bag of treasures in hand.

George, the owner, made the process easy for her, guiding her through the obituary, time of service the following evening, cremation and coffin expense already accounted for. He treated her like a close friend and took time to explain every detail of the ceremony. When they finished, his driver took her home to rest.

By the time she arrived home, Fred and Corinne were parked in front of the portico.

"Where were you, Mother? We were worried."

Exhausted, she took Fred's arm. "I was at Ferguson's Funeral Home making arrangements for tomorrow. Your father and I did business with George for years and today he reciprocated." Again Sharon felt shivers of grief start to overcome her. She tightened her grip on Fred and closed her eyes. Breathe and calm yourself. Barry's gone since yesterday. There are years ahead to get used to this emptiness. Or will I ever be strong without him?

"Where are the kids? I thought you all would stay overnight or longer."

"Uh, James is in the middle of SAT's and Lori is studying for midterms."

Astonished, she looked from her son to his wife. "Their grandfather dies and they can't get away to say goodbye?"

Sharon turned her back in disgust, unlocked the door, and entered the empty house. Welcome barks came from the yard. Fred and Corinne stayed put in the driveway.

"Are you coming in? It's too cold to leave the door open."

"Uh, no, Mother. We already checked into a motel a mile away. Corrine isn't fond of dogs."

"Oh. All right."

She ran upstairs, changed out of the gray silk dress and into jeans and a sweat shirt. Then she hurried down to let her pups in. They gave her more affection than she'd had from her own son. Wet kisses and a romp around the floor from the sweet big dogs brought more tears to her eyes. "Barry, what a mess I am without you. I haven't the training to be strong. I never even drove the car at night alone except when you were sick." More tears came with the sad memory. Be strong, dammit. Stand up for yourself. Just try it.

She called Fred's cell phone. He picked up. Before he had a chance to say a word, his mom spoke her mind. "You get my grandchildren here no later than tomorrow morning or they are out of the will and so are you." She pushed the end button. Brats are not going to treat us this way, my sweetheart. No way, no how.

# Chapter 4

Gracie and Tommy were a comfort all day, at her side guarding their mistress. Friends stopped by with different casseroles. Some just called to say hello. Sharon thanked them and noticed the women, all from the circle of friends, stayed close to their husbands during short visits. Puzzled, she felt friendship ebb away like a tide.

And suddenly it was night, almost twenty-four hours without Barry. Brakes screeched in the driveway, car doors opened and fresh air poured in with Jeff and Inge opening the unlocked front door. Hugs and kisses mixed with tears, English and Danish language combined. At last, they were here to guide her through the first stage of widowhood.

They tore into a casserole of pasta with meatballs followed by a hot shower for the travelers after a big romp with the dogs. "Our little dog Phistr would love these big poochies."

"My Danish grand dog." Sharon smiled. "I call him Feasta on Skype and he always perks up for Granny just as if he's one of the children. Your mom is taking care of them, I guess?"

"Along with our housekeeper, Malte. She's so good with them."

Jeff kissed his mom. "If you don't mind, we'll get some sleep. We can talk while I cook breakfast."

"Perfect. Now scoot and we'll all sleep."


The old hooty owl in the big oak tree Sharon and Barry always enjoyed so much had a sad hoot to his funny old voice as snowflakes fell.

Sharon hugged Barry's pillow and wished him farewell on his journey. Once again she spoiled the dogs and allowed them on the king-sized bed.

The next day it was to be ashes to ashes. How do you mend a broken heart? You must take one step and then another and another. The widow had lulled herself to sleep.


Coffee, bacon, and waffle aromas wafted through the house. Already the dogs were fed and outside. Content with her loved ones in the house, Sharon slipped into Barry's robe and hurried down the stairs. No one made waffles like her Jeff. Inge had set the table with flowers picked from several arrangements. Her artistic lovely daughter-in-law with long blond hair twisted in a braid, wore a stylish dress and a knitted angora pink scarf around her neck. She tied another loosely around her mother-in-law's slender neck

"Thank you, honey. This will keep me warm. I so love angora and you knitted this, didn't you?"

A shy hug from her daughter-in-law and they all prepared for the funeral.

Step by step, Sharon dressed. This isn't a party, she thought. The dress is pretty, my hair looks nice, the make-up is just enough, yet I'm shaking inside. My children are here.

Barry is lying dead in a box. This is the end, really the end of Act One of my life.

The funeral home was standing room only. Like a play, Sharon thought as her mind wandered. She couldn't focus on the funeral. Friends poured in to express condolences. Blah, blah, blah is the way it sounded to Sharon. She acknowledged voices in a daze. She sat and waited for Act One to end.

The family stood in front of the coffin that contained her husband. Each one kissed the father and grandfather's cold cheek. Sharon leaned over to whisper one last I love you. Jeff, so eloquent in his praise for his Dad, brought tears to the onlookers. He also introduced Inge and made everyone chuckle when he said, "She's Danish but she also speaks English so I won't have to translate if you want to chat."

Fred stepped forward, pulled a piece of paper from his pocket and read. "Father, I'm so sorry I caused you anxiety when I was a teenager. You and Mother always forgave me. I'll miss you so much and I promise to help Mother in every way I can."

Sharon winced at his phony words. Where was he when they needed help?

The grandchildren spoke well about the grandfather they hardly knew and expressed sadness.

The cynic in Sharon thought private school taught rhetoric very well.

Corrine complained of a sore throat. Instead of speaking, she placed a red rose in the casket.

The preacher, who knew the family well, spoke in glowing terms of Barry who always responded to the needs of the congregation. "Whether coaching a team or singing in the choir, I knew I could call on our beloved Barry Michaels. God Bless Him and keep him."

Act One had ended. Sharon knew she had to write Act Two herself and she had no idea how to accomplish that overwhelming task.


Customers stopped by to pay respects and one chose to use the moment to ask about business. Suddenly Fred was at his Mother's side. "Of course Mom and I will continue to give good service to all of our fine customers. We will need a few days to settle down and then we'll contact you."

We'll contact you? Her son knew nothing about their business except that it put food on the table and paid for college. Maybe he'd changed, grown up at last into manhood and meant his words. The kids had to return to Denmark soon and just for a minute, Fred comforted her. After all, he was the first born. She and Barry lavished love on their new baby from the day he was born. So why not give him a second chance. She needed Fred to help run the company. She'd teach him the trade and they'd continue to be successful. Michaels and Son. Could it be a daydream or reality?

# Chapter 5

The lovely old house filled with friends after the funeral. Conversations revolved around Barry's sunny disposition and how Jeff reflected the same personality. There were comments about Fred's good looks and his beautiful family that puffed up Sharon's older son. Corrine drove the children back to private school with a promise to return soon.

Private school? Again Sharon thought how come public school wasn't good enough and the expense. Well, it's not her business.

By late afternoon most everyone had left with a promise to keep in close touch. Sharon wondered if this were true. How would she fit with all the doubles now that she was single. Single. The very word brought more tears and a knowledge she didn't belong in a world where comfort and friendship filled part of every day.

A call came in from Denmark. Jeff frowned. When he finished speaking he told his mom they had to leave. Rasmus, the one of the prominent directors of the dance academy reported that chief dancer, Kulas, sprained her ankle and could not perform the next evening. That meant big trouble since the show had been sold out for weeks. They had to leave right away.

Forlorn and saddened by the news, Sharon kicked off her shoes and curled up on the couch. Soon all would be gone, the big house empty except for the dear canines and the widow. Yes, I'm the widow. Is life alone an adventure? She shook her head. No, definitely not. It's one day at a time to see what happens like a baby taking steps. Now she'd have to learn to live alone. If Fred works out in business, okay. If not, she'd advertise for someone with experience.

The doorbell rang. The urn came home. Jeff and Inge gathered her in their capable arms just in time. The package opened easily, the saddest she'd ever seen containing ashes of her precious husband. Is this where the hurting stopped? No, not yet. She handed her son a small bottle, no bigger than a medicine container, to fill and take with him to the small country where he and his family lived.

"Dad always liked to travel. His wish has come true. I'll take him wherever I go and make sure he's well taken care of."

"Mamse, we hate to leave you alone. The minute you change your mind, come live with us. Our little ones want to get to know you better and you will love our happy country. It is unique." And moments later the door closed. They were gone.

With tears held back when they left, Sharon thought she'd save them for another time. Now she had to fend for herself, figure things out and above all, she knew to watch out for Fred and his greedy family. The dogs panted in for food and consolation. Like big bookends they surrounded Sharon on the couch where she looked through an album of family photographs.

"See this one?" Tommy's sloppy tongue swiped her face. "Thanks, you silly pooch. This was taken when Barry and I met in high school. It was love at first sight like you and Gracie girl." The dog grunted as if he understood. Page after page she turned and soon icy fingers of fear filled Sharon with a sense of helplessness. Panic lanced her heart when she saw the wedding picture.

Then held back tears surfaced and dripped to roll down her cheeks and be lapped by her canine pals; her only friends so close at hand. When does it end? I must get hold of myself. After wiping the album, she put on winter clothes and boots and put leashes on the big pups. "Time to stop being lazy. A walk at night is good, right? They sat, wagging long tails to agree. Out they went in the cold night. Just damn do it.

A quick wave to the next door neighbor who rolled out the trash barrel reminded Sharon of another chore. Okay, I can do it. Just make a list and call someone to shovel snow and clean off the driveway. That's what I can do and right away. A stumble on an ice chunk sent her flying into a snow bank.

"Help. Help me." The neighbor, Bill Hughes, came running, slowed when he saw the big dogs growling.

"What can I do, Sharon? Will they bite? Command them or something."

"Sit, Stay," she said in a loud firm voice. "Bill, come to me without fear. I'll reach out to you and take hold of your arm so you can lift me to a standing position. Then back up when I tell you."

With care, the frightened man did as told and together, under the watchful eyes of two large dogs, Sharon got to a standing position. She took a deep breath and noticed her neighbor did, too. "Bill, I owe you one."

White breath puffs of wintry cold came from every mouth. "I need someone to shovel. Do you have a name for me?"

"Oh yes. I can do it. I have a blower and can easily manage your driveway and that walk as well as mine. Is Barry okay? I haven't seen him lately."

She stared at him. He doesn't know. "I'm devastated, Bill. He died a few days ago."

The instinct when you hear news like that is to embrace the person and that's exactly what Bill Hughes did. Again the dogs went on high alert. Again Sharon's muffled voice told them to sit and stay. And the neighbors held each other for a long while to bring a touch of solace to the widow.

"Thanks, Bill. I needed that. Now if I can walk back to my house without falling, I'll be okay."

"I'd like to walk you right to the door for safety's sake if you don't mind."

And they made it without incident. Sharon thanked him for saving her and decided on the spur of the moment to invite Bill and his wife to dinner in a couple of weeks.

"No wife. No more. She left last year, ran off with another man. The kids are grown and I have the house. I still have a good position at the university where I teach creative writing. Full classes every year. Think over your invitation and when you're ready, ask me again. I have some excellent wine." He bent over and touched his lips to her damp cheeks.

"Thanks for saving me. I will call."

In the house, all locked up, she knew she needed to talk to Barry. After brushing her dogs and wiping them dry with a big towel, Sharon gave each of them a dog biscuit treat and the three of them climbed the stairs. Sharon soaked in the hot tub to soothe her sore body and eventually felt better. A bit of lotion rubbed in and on her skin, clean pajamas and in the mirror, she began what became a nightly dialogue with her deceased husband.

"Honey, you recall our neighbor Bill Hughes, the college professor." She smoothed La Mer on her skin oh so gently. "Well, it's a long story but tonight I fell walking the poochies and Bill picked me up so sweet and I'll skip to the end but he gave me a tiny kiss on my cheek. My question is do you mind?" From the bedroom, Sharon heard a crash. She ran in to find a lamp overturned. Tommy and Gracie were curled in their own big beds in the corner of the room, asleep. "Is that your answer, Barry? I'll follow your lead." She slept very well that cold night.

Mia, the housekeeper showed up the next day with a pan full of blueberry muffins. They had breakfast together before Mia got busy. Sharon bundled up, took remains from the urn to spread them around bushes they planted thirty years before. With tender loving care, Sharon sprinkled some close to the roots of peonies and so many more bushes, she couldn't recall their names. Snow melted under her boots so careful not to fall, she went back in the house, the dogs behind her.

The phone rang. Fred was calling. "I'm ready to pitch in Mother. Show me how the business runs on a daily basis."

A few days alone made Sharon feel needy. She considered a son, tall and good looking so like his father to drive with on calls to clients. A burden lifted when he arrived; she hugged him.

"Let's go in the office where I can explain a few things. The business isn't complicated. You measure the space carefully, show the client cabinet samples and deliver on time. We don't install. There are several companies we work with so measuring is very important."

"Oh, it sounds easy enough and after installation, we bill the client."

"Right. We've been doing this for years. I have a system."

"So where are the rulers and let's get started."

Sharon reached into the closet to withdraw several sizes of special measuring tools.

"Whoa." Fred backed off. "I've never seen devices like these. I pictured the regular 12 inch rulers."

"Well, my son, if we are to be partners, you better learn fast."

He whined. "Uh maybe you can hire a guy to measure."

A mother is patient, more than patient. "Fred, go to the local hardware store and ask the manager. Introduce yourself and tell him you need to learn right away. Then come back and we'll see. Watch, listen and learn, otherwise we have no business. I'll close up."

"And live on the insurance money?"

A vein throbbed in her forehead. Sharon touched it and knew aspirin and ice would help when her son left.

"Any money I have is my business. Please learn the simple task of measuring and we can move on. Right now I must lie down. Come back later with good news, Fred."

After locking the door, Sharon did the ice and aspirin and thought about her son's behavior. Dumb or lazy, take your pick, mother. Neither worked for her. If he comes back empty handed and whining, she'd close or sell the business.

Her life appeared to have a pattern now. Lock the door, answer the phone, talk to the pups, try to sleep. Sure enough, the phone rang. Their good pal, Howard, the insurance man, had something for her. All the years of fighting with him about payments and different plans might finally come to fruition.

"Come right over, Howie. I could use some good news."

Soon the energetic, personable man she and Barry met years before, arrived. They sat in the living room where flowers wilted just like the new widow.

"It's a sad time without Barry here but that's what insurance is all about. Over the years we planned you'd be taken care of if he passed on before you. Here's the total check and it is substantial, Sharon. Barry meant it for you only and he advised me to see that you invested the money with one of three companies. Either one will protect your investment and counsel you." He handed her three cards; one had a smiley face on it from Howie to show his choice.

She twisted her wedding ring and stared at the check. "So this is what it's all about. All the planning to take care of me in case. Now I won't have to bag groceries or wait on customers at Macy's."

Sharon's old friend patted her hand. "Barry wanted the best for you. I've never seen a closer couple than the two of you. How about this? I'll drive you to the bank where you sign the check and make the deposit. Then it's safe overnight until you decide about the investor." He winked giving Sharon another clue.

"Thanks, my friend. It's a good plan."Again she locked the door and with handbag in hand, off she went in his car to protect her future.

Later they waved goodbye and back she went into a day to day life without Barry. There were decisions to be made about investors even though Howie preferred one by drawing a smiley face. Her body felt limp like a Raggedy Ann Doll and Jeff so far away with his own life to live, a business to run, a wife and children to take care of. I only have me. I don't even drive at night. So do it, you ninny. You're fifty six, old enough. Old enough for what?

The worst idea she had all day was when she decided to look in the mirror. Self-assessment, she called it. My skin's good inherited from Mom and that's a big help for an aging woman. Maybe I'll start having facials every month, walk more on the treadmill and use the bike to nowhere. By spring, she'll feel better. Barry still gone but there's nothing to do about that.

# Chapter 6

Just when she gave up on Fred, he knocked on the door, Corrine by his side. "I should have a key, Mother. What if something happens to you and..."

She stopped him from rattling on. "Good morning to you both. Fred, I do have an emergency bracelet for help ever since the hip surgery. And there's always 911. Come in. The dogs are in the yard."

Fred went straight to the fridge and searched for anything, an old habit she despised.

"Can I get you something?"

"Uh coffee or best a soda with caffeine."

"Sit down, both of you. Something's on your minds so speak up."

"Okay, Mother."

"And Fred, I'm your mom. So please be less formal and call me Mom. And I mean both of you"

"Okay, uh Mom. Here's the deal. You see Corrine took shop in school and has a lot of know-how with tools and uh stuff like measuring tools. My idea is that Corrine becomes part of the company. She'll be the measuring guy and you and I will see uh, clients."

"Really, Corrine, you know your way around tools?"

"Oh sure. I had lots of experience in the old wood shop classes."

"Follow me to the office. I'll show you the rulers we've used for years. In our business, measuring accurately is the key to sales."

Fred hunkered around the door while Sharon showed Corrine the tools.

"You bet." Her blond daughter-in-law handled them similar to the way Barry had.

"Measure the kitchen cabinet as if I'm a customer who wants a new cabinet."

With confidence, Corrine swayed her hips over and did the job.

"Good job and very professional, Corinne."

"Thanks, Mom."

"Look, I have an appointment soon. Can you come back in a few hours? We can have lunch here."

Corinne elbowed Jeff and they said okay and drove off.

Sharon had some thinking to do.

She drove to World Wide Investors where concentration on her funds was difficult. The big boss, a large hearty man, smothered the wealthy widow with compliments on running a successful business for many years. He discussed how her money would be invested. Two younger men produced charts, explained how the company's plan worked and the final words had to do with their take on all their clever work.

All Sharon thought was that she needed Barry because she hadn't a clue as to what they were saying. They're the money men. How could a widow make sense of their money speak?

After signing the contract, she noticed her hands shook. Not the old steady signature from two weeks ago.

Snow fell fast when Sharon left. No kind gentleman ran out to clean off her car. What the hell? Now that they had her money, they were though with Sharon Michaels. Brush in hand, she struggled to clean off the windows and the rest of the car. A few buttons pushed and a warm climate comforted her chilled body. Weary, her mending hip not happy, Sharon made her way home to find the driveway and walk cleaned of snow. Thanks a bunch, dear neighbor. He definitely deserves a dinner soon.

Into the garage she pulled with a big decision ahead. But first the pets needed to come in from their comfortable big heated dog house. They barked loud and happy to see her at first sight. After wiping them dry, bowls of food were set out and she made her way upstairs to change into warm sweats. Thoughts flitted in and around her mind. If she allowed Fred and Corrine into the company, it would be two against one when any decisions were made. On the other hand, they might be a big help. It would be good for them and her to grow the business.

1. They live in a rental in New Jersey. Too far to commute or good to spread the business?

2. What about Fred's small company? Bankrupt or what's the status? Ask.

3. Private school? How does that work and how can they afford it?

"Oh, Barry, who can I turn to for advice. Maybe Howie, huh? He's the only one I can think of. Our former friends apparently don't like single women. There's no room for me, then. Not too nice after twenty years of closeness. She thought of having an open discussion with some of them and shook her head. The investment contract went into a file cabinet where she kept all personal information.

When the doorbell rang, Sharon figured there were many adjustments about to be made if their small family would work well together.

"Who shoveled the driveway, Mom?"

She laughed to think of all the times teen aged Fred refused to help causing aggravation years ago. Now he noticed. "Bill Hughes, our next door neighbor who has promised to help out through the winter. He's a professor at Nyack University."

"Wow. Well I'll do it any time."

After wet boots were removed, sweet smiles crossed attractive faces ready to talk business. What a change, Sharon thought. Fred and Corinne wore matching white shirts under suit jackets, very business-like. They had a professional look about them. What a far cry from the first visit.

"Me and Corinne are excited about joining your company. Let's talk about how it works. You and Dad were a great team. You made a lot of money. We bet with the three of us, we can double sales."

With those words, Fred had a triumphant expression on his face. The genius speaks.

Sharon, as the mother, felt her heart sing with their enthusiasm. "Doubling sales sounds great. How do we accomplish that?"

Corrine jumped in. "I'm good with customer service, making friends and stuff while I measure. We have a lot of contacts in New Jersey like contractors and builders. Fred can set up meetings and we go from there."

"So what you're saying is I'll continue with New York contacts. Construction is at an all-time high right now. This sounds good. Will you stay in New Jersey?" She didn't miss the look they exchanged.

"No, the lease is up. We'll find a place in New York. Do you have any suggestions, Mom?"

"Not right now. Check Real Estate to see what's available and what about the children's school?"

"They'll stay until June if we find a good high school nearby."

"That shouldn't be a problem."

"Well, Mom, it seems we have the semblance of a company. Working hard together we can and will succeed. Michaels and Company." They all shook hands and the new members left due to the heavy snowfall. Sharon watched them pull away, happy smiles on their faces and wondered if somehow her son and his wife had put one over on her. How come the meeting went so smooth and friendly or had her son and daughter-in law planned something to pull on the dumb trusting mother.

Disturbed without knowing why, Sharon decided not to call Jeff. Instead she searched for her neighbor's card and called him.

"Bill, it's Sharon. Thanks so much for plowing my driveway. Are you busy now or plainly speaking, would you like to have dinner over here?"

43

"Sharon, how delightful. Yes and what time? "

"I'll check the kitchen and see what I can put together. I haven't shopped since um, well you understand."

His manly chuckle so like Barry's brought tears to her eyes.

"Loneliness can drag you down but a friendly dinner is just the thing to perk us up on this snowy night. How about I bring something tasty from my kitchen and you make a salad. I'll be over in about an hour. Does that work for you, my dear?"

She sighed. Bill, almost a stranger, just took charge and made life more pleasant. "Yes, an hour is perfect. See you then."

She fed the dogs and sent them out to their snug house just in case Bill didn't care for her big canines roaming around. Then she took a refreshing shower and picked out casual clothes . She dressed in a maroon sweater and fitted tan pants, brushed her hair loose and fluffy. She added the finishing touch, a silk scarf with blended colors.

All the while she thought about Barry. "Honey, he's a nice man and I'm lonely. Maybe I can talk about my business concerns."

The fixings for a terrific salad were fresh. Romaine lettuce, tomatoes, red onions, black olives, one ripe avocado and blue cheese grated. Barry's favorite. No tears, she warned herself. Slice, dice, cut and soon, in two wooden salad bowls, a very attractive entrée sat ready to consume. Without a care as to what Bill had in mind, she set the table and added two ivory candles in silver candle sticks. The fireplace needed a twist of a knob to light. She glanced around at the old living room, so pretty and warm.

The door bell rang. Excitement filled her as she hurried to open the door. "Hi Bill, right on time."

"Sharon, it's so good to see you on your feet and looking so beautiful." Bill set a shopping bag down, removed his coat and hugged her.

Flustered, Sharon lifted the bag and brought it to the kitchen.

"Allow me." Bill lifted a wrapped roasted chicken and set it on the counter. "There's more." Sharon couldn't help herself from giggling as Bill placed little packs of red potatoes, steamed spinach and mushrooms next to the chicken.

"What a treat. I haven't eaten much since Barry died and now real food. You're an angel, Bill."

"And you, lovely lady, concocted a delightful salad. Let's have a drink, red or white, I brought both."

"You're spoiling me, Bill. White."

He poured the wine into some elegant glasses she brought out and they sipped, the atmosphere perfect for just grown-ups after dealing with possible scheming children. Sharon asked Bill about his work. Interested to find out about creative writing and the fact he'd written many published books, spy stories filled with romance and intrigue. He sliced the chicken like a pro and dished out small portions of food for both of them. Wine flowed as she kept him talking. After dinner they moved to the couch in the living room where the fire warmed the room.

A bit tipsy, Sharon kicked off her shoes and curled up in a corner. Bill edged in close to her and casually placed an arm around her shoulder.

45

"Bill, I'm very comfortable with you so would you mind if I confide something. I don't have anyone to discuss this with."

"I've spent the entire dinner talking your head off. Now it's your turn. What's on your mind?"

The fire flickered across his earnest face. Sharon felt she might trust him. "Barry and I had a successful company, just the two of us. Now I'm alone. Suddenly my oldest son, an unsuccessful man, sad to say, and his odd, kind of nasty wife, have turned into sweet and charming kids who want to be partners with me. Today they came over with a well thought out business plan and when they left, all smiley faced, I had the feeling they might have, well, the words are harsh, they 'put something over on the old lady'."

Quiet for a while, finally Bill spoke. "Go with your inner feeling, Sharon. You need help with the business but watch them with care. Make sure the orders they write are perfect and honest. Keep track and if something seems off kilter, let's talk again. Do not sign a contract with them." He shook his head. "I wish you well. Very well." With that, he pulled her close and gave her a kiss hot enough to melt her nail polish. And she kissed her neighbor right back with fervor enough they didn't need the fireplace heat. She tasted dinner in his kisses and shivered. When his hands roamed, she had to stop. Too much, too soon for the new widow.

Bill had trouble walking when he left soon after. She'd seen the same reaction many times from Barry and even her sons. They agreed to have dinner again soon, very soon. Singing 'Don't Stop Thinking About Tomorrow, Yesterday's gone,' Sharon brought Tommy and Gracie in for the night. Since Bill helped clean up after dinner, all Sharon had to do was get to bed. She thought of his advice and found it to be sound. What a night! Satisfied with good company and a few kisses, she crawled under the comforter and fell asleep.

# Chapter 7

As tired as he was, Jeff still wanted to speak to his mom. Too much time passed since they were with her and he wondered how she was getting through each day.

"Mom, finally we're connected. Wait just a darn minute. You look good so I guess you're making it day by day."

"Jeffie, I'm so happy to see your face. How did the big show work out with the primo dancer injured?"

"Cool. The new girl has talent, triple threat. She sings, dances, acts. Every show sold out. Our company is expanding. Big dollars to feed the munchkins And speaking of big dollars, how is business? It must be difficult to work alone."

Sharon held her breath before telling him the latest arrangements or rather a version of what's going on.

"Since it's impossible to continue working the company with just me alone, your brother and his wife offered to help out. Corinne is good in the measurement department having taken woodshop and Fred can develop business in New Jersey while I continue with our old customers in this area."

Jeff's face turned into a storm cloud. "I knew it. The minute I turned my back he jumped in to see if he can become a partner. Oh, Shit. Sorry, Mom. He's a snake so beware. Watch the company checkbook. Listen to me. Here's the scenario I see. First they'll help grow the business. You'll be happy and relax . After a while you'll examine the checkbook and notice he's written a check for an item have nothing to do with business."

"Jeff, what do you mean?"

"For instance, Corinne needs her teeth fixed. Haven't you noticed she has bad teeth? Believe me, they are not to be trusted. Did you get the insurance money?"

"Yes and it's safe with an investment company Howie recommended."

"Thank God for that. What else has brought a smile to your beautiful face, Mom?"

Sharon heard her grandchildren singing before bed time and wished she were in Denmark to hold them.

"Well. Um my next door neighbor saved me from a bad fall and now he's plowing the driveway."

"And what else about this neighbor?"

"He came over for dinner last night. It was um, very pleasant."

"Mommy, beware of new men in your life and watch out for Fred and his wife. Right now, I'm too tired to think about all the ways I can protect you. Love from Inge. Goodnight."

And her image disappeared just like that.

Inge entered the bedroom pleased the children went down without complaint." What's going on, honey? Did you speak with Mamse?"

"Get in bed and hold me tight."

Inge obliged. "Was that Mom on Skype?"

"Oh yeah. First of all, my older brother and his wife have wormed their way into Mom and Dad's company. I told her what to watch for. Then Mom's next door neighbor came over for dinner last night and, Inge, Mom had a sweet smile on her face just now. I warned her about men and bad sons and now I'm too tired to think. It's like having a teen ager to watch over."

"We'll have to persuade her to move in with us before she gets in trouble, my love."

All Inge heard was the gentle snore of sleep from her troubled husband.

Dinners with Bill brought a new energy into Sharon's life. With his help over a few evenings, she sorted out a plan as to running the expanded company. She ordered more cabinet samples and invoices and planned weekly meetings at noon to check on work accomplished. Also she had to make sure expenses were legitimate like gas bills, lunches ,and phone calls. She'd take notes on new customers and progress. Bill suggested Sharon go over the checkbook carefully to make sure Fred didn't abuse the privilege.

"Oh, Bill, Fred would never do that. The checkbook's in my name."

"Yes, but now you had it changed to Michaels and Company. I'm warning you to beware."

On the way to bed, Sharon had her nightly chat with Barry. "Honey, I've always been a softie when it came to the children. Our Jeff turned out to be a huge success and a fine son. Fred, well I'm worried about him. He married a bitch and they can't be trusted."

49

Her slim arms clutched her body to give support. Weary, she closed her eyes and hoped she'd made the right business decision.

A movie came close to a break-up.

"Bill, I can't be seen with another man yet. It's too soon."

His eyes glared with a scary glow. "You're being old fashioned, Sharon. No one expects you to be a stay at home because you're a widow. Three months have gone by since he passed. Barry wouldn't want you to be alone."

He paced the floor while Sharon wrung her hands and wished she were somewhere else not having this stupid conversation going nowhere. "Bill, be sensible. You're wrong. I'm sorry. Maybe I am old fashioned."

He breathed hard before speaking. "Okay, I'll give you one more week and then we go public." He edged in for a kiss. "And frankly, I'm tired of just hugs and kisses. Think about it, Sharon."

He poured a glass of wine and drank it all. "So what's going on with the business, to change the subject?"

She brightened, happy he appeared to settle down. Sex with Bill was out of the question. She still belonged to Barry. A new bottle of Pinot Grigio was opened by Bill who poured two glasses full. They made a toast and relaxed. "Business is good so far. I'm keeping close tabs on everything you and I talked about. Corinne missed a few days of work for some unknown reason. Best of all, it's spring. No more plowing for you, my dear neighbor."

# Chapter 8

Business picked up. Sales boomed with new customers in New Jersey as winter came to a close. Every week, Michaels and Company met for a meeting. Fred and Corinne had leased an apartment not far from Sharon. They needed more cabinet samples to display, a good sign, and brought invoices to show and discuss with the boss. After all, Sharon knew what's what after years of running the company.

On one hand, she had a good feeling about what the young couple accomplished. On the other hand, she noticed a physical change in Corrine and finally figured out she'd had a boob job. Her thoughts raced to the checkbook. Surgery is expensive. How did they pay for it? She reached into the center drawer of her desk and pulled out the business checkbook. Thumbing through, there it was a paid bill to a doctor in New Jersey for Breast Augmentation.

"What's this all about?" Sharon turned the checkbook around for them to clearly see.

"Corinne needed augmentation a month ago. We'll pay you back next month. I didn't think you'd mind since we're doing so well in business."

"What do you mean by she needed augmentation. She wanted something so you opened the drawer and helped yourself to money? Well that's not the way business works here, Fred and you, Corinne. You work and get a salary. You live off the money you earn."

They exchanged looks as if they were naughty kids. "Oh. You never explained that to us when we joined the company."

"I see." Sharon sighed. "Maybe it's because it's new for me to handle a business and hire people. Your dad had died and I just tried to figure how it all works." She held her head in her hands. "Okay. Let's start from scratch and this time we'll get it right." She bit her tongue not willing to dig into past anger and mistakes. "You're starting over in a good family business. So don't take from your mother. Got it? I'll give you two months to pay me the money you took." Sharon, hands shaking with anger looked back at the check. Three thousand dollars. Oh my God. This is the worst case scenario. "Let's sit down and figure out how you can pay the company back."

Corinne opened her big mouth. "You got enough insurance money to last you forever." She swaggered out and slammed the door.

Stunned to hear those words from Corinne, she looked at Fred. "Please bring her back. We're family. Sometimes we say what we don't mean. I know Corinne doesn't have a mother. I hoped we'd grow closer. Fred, it's up to you to mend torn fences." Her son scowled and stomped out of the room the same way he'd done as a child. Do they ever grow up?

What should I do, Barry? In truth, they stole my money, the company's money.

They were back in a few minutes. Corinne wrapped her arms around Sharon as if she meant it. "Let's start again, Mom. We're sorry about everything, me and my big mouth and taking the money. We should've asked for a loan. It's something I always wanted and life's been so tough the past few years."

"Okay, let's make it painless. Small increments until you're paid off and you do look very nice. They hugged and left.

Fred and Corinne drove off in a Ford Explorer, an expensive SUV. Sharon quick scanned the check book and found a check written to a local Ford Dealer for a lot of money just yesterday. She dialed the number.

"The manager, please."

"Grant, this is Sharon Michaels. Yes, Barry's wife. I'm sorry to say our son Fred purchased a Ford Explorer without permission using our business check yesterday. I want you to stop payment and take the car back."

"Mrs. Michaels, it's a good thing you called. We'll stop payment and get our people to take the car back. Let me know if there's anything else I can do for you."

Humiliated and beyond sad, Sharon sobbed her heart out. She called Bill.

"Sorry, dear, I'm tutoring one of my students right now." She heard a giggle in the background as he hung up.

She called Fred. "A Ford Explorer is way too expensive, Fred. Be sensible. The Ford Company is coming over to take back the car. You can take a look at a smaller, less expensive car and somehow, the company will pay for it." She hung up and held her sad head. Bill is gone screwing some coed. Her family is taking advantage of her because she's a dumb widow. What happens next? Tears flowed once again. She has no husband, no decent family close by and no hot neighbor.

Thumbing through the local paper, she realized Barry was the one who read the evening news, talked it over with her, and explained when she didn't understand world situations. In all their years together, she didn't have a girlfriend; Sharon had Barry. A glance at every wall displayed tennis trophies where they played doubles tournaments and always won. Pictures with happiness shining from their faces from the day they met in high school right through to the last "I love you." What next?

A turn of the page and there she found an announcement. The New City library, close to home, this very night had the first Widow's Club gathering. Hmm. Of course, there must be more widows nearby. What a perfect way to get acquainted. She read more.

Different events were scheduled every week. Next month a local author would attend and lead a discussion titled Everyone Has a Story, Memoirs. This caught her interest. She decided she'd sign up for this one.

After the night feeding of her best pals, Gracie and Tommy, Sharon had a salad and searched her closet. The pink ruffled shirt and pressed jeans looked just right. Okay, sneakers or sandals, which one for comfort? After trying on one of each, Sharon decided to go for comfort and wore her favorite white sneaks. Off she drove worried as she went alone. Another hurdle to get used to since Barry died. She bet women of today drove alone, made their own decisions, married or not. Women even had children later in life. Sharon shook her head at that concept.

Ten minutes later she arrived safe, parked without crashing into another car, carried herself as if she did this all the time. Look out world, here comes the new improved Sharon Michaels. Warren, a friendly guy, always helpful from the check-out section, showed her where to go.

"Follow the signs downstairs and grab a chair. They're hoping for a crowd tonight."

She did as told, slid into one of the last chair just as a gavel hit the table.

"Ladies, welcome to the first meeting of the Widow's Club. Sign up on the chart at your table. I'm certain we have women from all over the county seeking friendships with other widow's. My name is Kathy Chambers, widowed for a year. If you're curious, I'll reveal I've been dating. Do what you like to do and you'll meet someone with common interests. It works for me."

A murmur went through the crowded room. Sharon knew each widow must have different thoughts about dating, second time around marriages, all unthinkable to her. The few dinners and a kiss or too with Bill Hughes meant nothing except filling a gap. No one would ever take Barry's place in her heart.

Again the gavel pounded for attention. Kathy grinned. "Shocked some of you, didn't I? Oh, how I love the power." A shake of her head changed the mood of the tall vivacious woman. "I'm over-compensating tonight. Maybe because I'm so pleased at the turnout here. I'd like our Widow's Cub to be a huge success but let me caution all of you, it does take work. Personally, I've longed for female friendships even though I'm dating. That said, let's move on, gals and welcome to the New City Library. We're thrilled to have the first meeting filled with enthusiastic women. Next month, a local well known author, Charmaine Gordon, has graciously consented to teach a seminar. She's known for her survive and thrive stories, Romance and Suspense and mature books. Her motto is "it isn't over 'til it's over." She's a mighty optimistic woman. I'm looking forward to meeting her."

"What's next right now, Kathy?" The woman to the right of Sharon called out.

"What's next is we play getting to know you. So turn to the woman to the right of you and share something about your life since becoming a widow. Go."

Sharon turned to face the woman who spoke up before. Her pleasant face had an eager expression as if she couldn't wait to listen.

"Hi, I'm Sharon Michaels. Widowhood sucks." She looked around and said to herself, did I really say that?

Her partner of the moment burst into laughter. Sharon's face turned red.

"Sorry, I've never used that word before but it's true. To lose your best friend, your husband, really sucks."

Applause and laughter filled the room.

"You're one honest lady, Ms. I feel the same way." Kathy banged the gavel. "What a great start. What's your name back there. Stand up so we can all see you."

"Sharon Michaels. My Barry and I were best pals, in business together, tennis partners so I never cultivated women friends. Who knew he'd be gone too soon so here I am."

"You broke the ice, Sharon. Let's continue around each table. If anyone has skills we can develop in the club, speak up or write them down with your name, number and town. I bet we have a lot of widows from more than Rockland County."

"Orange County here." One hand raised from a woman in a green shirt. Nyack, Westchester and so it went. There were widows from all over seeking friendship.

Kathy wrote on the blackboard fast as she could, a big grin on her face. "Ladies, our goal is to make friends. Common interests help form strong bonds. That's where skills come in."

"I love to read. My name is Debbie, remember me with the white hair 'cause I can organize a book club to meet once a month and stick to it."

"Thanks Debbie with the beautiful white hair." Kathy wrote it down

Two women held up their hands. "I am Roopa and my friend Naushin are good with anything to do with yarn. We knit, weave, crochet, do crafts of all kind and novices are welcome to learn. It's peaceful and fun."

"We have two talented ladies. Thank you." Again Kathy wrote it on the blackboard. She spun around and pointed to a younger woman with black spiky hair. "Andrea, girlfriend, don't hide. Folks, she has a background in singing, playing with bands, good on drums and guitar, a musical wizard. If anyone wants to start a band, she's the one to lead."

Three women jumped to their feet hands raised. "We've been trying to do this for years. We're in."

"That's Great. We'll get a show together to entertain for the elderly and possibly returned warriors, veterans at West Point, and kids with developmental disabilities. The possibilities are endless."

Soon everyone gathered around the pastry table, coffee in hands, chatting away. Sharon felt better than she had in months. She'd think about where she'd fit in and call. The drive home seemed a whole lot shorter than getting there.

# Chapter 9

Work dragged on Monday. Sharon met with customers, made sales and by the end of the day, she didn't know if working without a partner was the best thing to fill her life. Empty, she felt empty. A change of clothes and she piled the eager pets in the car for fun at the dog park. Spring brought out the best in people with canines. Tongues hung out the back window. They strained at the leashes until Sharon let Tommy and Gracie loose behind the fence. Before long, other folks showed up with different sized canines. Sharon had to laugh at a fierce Chihuahua barking at her large pets. The owner, a man dressed in a suit, joined her.

"Come here often?" His voice deep and musical.

"That's a line from a bar, right?"

"Yes, it is. I used it a lot in the old days. It worked most of the time."

"I never bar hopped. I married young and lost my husband a few months ago. How about you?"

"I'm married to this pip squeak pet of mine the past few years. Janis Joplin is her name. She can't sing but man, can she bark in High C. I was divorced a couple of times before then. I just can't seem to get it right."

"Tommy, Gracie, NO!" Sharon's dogs stopped harassing another canine. "They've been in the back yard too long without my attention. I'll have to bring them here more often."

The tall stranger smiled. "I hope you do. What's your name, if you don't mind."

She searched his face for a clue as to his personality. How can you tell at first glance? She had so little experience with just about everything.

He touched her cheek rosy with the chilly spring breeze. "I'm Jack Torrance. I sing on Broadway right now in a revival of Chicago. Now it's your turn and remember, I'm just asking for your name."

"Sharon Michaels. My husband and I have a business, not very exciting. Now I sell kitchen cabinets and my oldest son and his wife joined the company to help me. Today, Jack," she tested his name on her tongue, "I felt way out of sorts about visiting customers on my own so I packed up the pups we rescued a few years ago and here we are."

"Good job, Sharon. We're having a conversation. This isn't too painful, is it?"

"No. It's just different. Tell me about your career."

He laughed. "It's checkered, at best. I've been a song and dance man forever, sometimes scoring a good part, sometimes chorus. As long as I keep working, have union benefits, I'm good. I live in Tappan, not far from here in a small cottage where I can hit the Palisade Parkway and get to town fast."

The wind picked up and Sharon shivered. "It's time to head home." She called to the dogs and turned to Jack. "Would you like to have dinner at my house now. Monday's you're off, right?"

"Why thank you, yes I'd love to. That's brave of you."

"Yes, it is. I need company and you're just the one. Follow me."

Jack tucked Janis in her little dog house and started up his Volkswagon.

Sharon rounded up her two rowdy pups and home she went with her new friend behind her. "Barry, what in the world did I just do? Is it weird to invite a relative stranger to our home? Yeah, it is. I'll keep a knife handy. You're the one in heaven. It's lonely down here without you."

Fast, she fed the dogs and sent them out to the yard while Jack waited in his car.

"Now what do we do with Janis?"

"She'll sleep in her little house in the car while we have dinner."

Into the house they went where he stopped to admire her taste. "Sharon, this is so cozy and comfortable. I'm guessing you've lived here many years." He ran his long fingers over the piano. "Do you play?"

She blushed admitting the truth to a real performer. "Not often and not too well. Why?"

Color came to his cheeks. "I have an opportunity for the part of Amos who sings Cellophane in Chicago. I know the song so well and the dance but I'd love to have someone help me practice and critique what I'm doing."

Sharon took a deep breath. "I haven't played in a long time. Do you have sheet music? Maybe I'd be able to help. I always did for my boys."

Jack swept her into a dance move and hugged her just right. "You're a doll. I have music in the car. You fix something easy for dinner and I'll get my portfolio." He raced to the door and left her open mouthed surprised.

What a kick to meet an actor and bring him home for dinner. Am I having fun or what? In the fridge she found salad, deviled eggs Mia made with black olives on the side and avocado slices. Sherbet to cleanse the palate in the freezer and some left over crème brulee. Hmm. Just enough for a light meal.

By the time Jack hurried in, the table was set. Excited to show her the music and begin, Sharon told him to calm down and have a bite or two. Then they'd check out what else he carried in his portfolio.

Small eater, she thought, or too anxious to settle down but she enjoyed every bit of the light dinner. When they finished, he rushed to the piano and played while Sharon cleared the table. She joined him in the living room where he apologized for not helping. Eyes sparkling, he handed her the sheet music for Cellophane and stood up ready to sing.

"Hang on a minute, Jack. Let me bumble my way through first."

To Sharon's surprise, she caught on right away. Two or three times over the music and soon Jack sang as she played. His voice clear and touching as he sang the words about how nobody knows my name. Dance movement came with it. Obviously he'd worked on the audition for hours.

"So what do you think?"

"Poignant. I'd like to see you relax a bit more in the dance when you kind of shimmy, reach out to the audience; start softer with your voice and build on it. But Jack, what do I know? One thing for sure, you touched me with the way you sang as if it was the truth. Nobody knows your name. You made me want to cry. Sing as if this happens to you on a daily basis, make it believable. You're not just a song and dance man anymore. You're special. I mean it."

"Sharon," he kneeled at her feet, "you may be the best thing that ever happened to me in years."

"Let me know what happens, my friend."

"I'll send you tickets." He hugged Sharon and hurried out the door.

"What just happened, Barry? I took the pups to the dog park, met an actor, invited him home and played the piano for him so he'd audition plus I gave him critique on how to perform it better. All the years I spent in your dear shadow and here I am giving advice to an actor." Sharon laughed and didn't stop. Maybe she was Cellophane all this time.

Three days later, red roses arrived with two tickets to Chicago. Sharon called Kathy Chambers to invite her to the play.

# Chapter 10

A red Benz zoomed into Sharon's driveway right on time. Out slid Kathy, dressed in a hot red silk short tunic, spiked heels and her crowning glory mane of hair loose around bare shoulders, a shawl around her neck.

"Quick, Kathy. Use your magic wand to change me into someone grand like you. Otherwise I'll feel dowdy by your side."

Giggling like school girls, they raced upstairs to Sharon's closet where Kathy took over. The click of hangers filled the room as Kathy slid one outfit after another until she held up a dress Sharon never wore. Too tight, too short, too bright and Barry liked it.

"Try this. Pink is so pretty and with your blond hair, yum."

One twirl around in the mirror and Sharon knew her friend had picked the right dress.

"You're my fashion consultant from now on. No more old fashioned me."

"Oh hush, we're having fun. Brush your hair, use shine spray and let's get going. We don't want to miss the overture." With confidence, Kathy got to the Palisade Parkway and relaxed at the wheel. "I'm excited to see Chicago. You'll have to tell me how this evening came to be."

Sharon began with meeting Jack and his tiny dog Janis Joplin, at the dog park. That brought a big laugh from both of them.

"Wait a minute, by chance you refreshed your skill at the piano enough to help Jack audition and get the part?"

"Uh, yes. I don't have much experience in piano or theater but there it was when I least expected it."

Kathy drove on, quiet for a while, less animated.

"What's on your mind or have you run out of steam?"

"I'm a high school teacher with a lot of insight into my kids. You knocked me for a loop when you said widowhood sucks at the Widow's Club meeting. You look like Clark Kent, a mild mannered reporter who turns into Superman."

Sharon roared with laughter. "Who me?"

"Yeah. I think you're coming out of a cocoon to reveal a butterfly with talent hidden for many years in the guise of good mom, good wife, good partner." Kathy reached over to touch her friend's hand. "Sharon Michael's, I so appreciate the opportunity to be friends with you."

Satisfaction and pride filled the former lonely widow. She'd found her first lady friend.


Third row center were the best tickets and the only seats in the packed house where theater goers dressed up. Not like the days of old where a trip to Broadway required your best clothes. Sharon felt glamorous in pink with her gorgeous friend in red.

The show glittered with out-of-this-world costumes, and when Jack did his rendition of Cellophane, he brought the house down. No more song and dance man only. A star was born.

Kathy whispered, "Outstanding and you are amazing. I have plans for you."

Afterward, the women went backstage. Jack embraced Sharon and did a double take at her titian haired friend. Besieged by admirers, he didn't have much time to chat.

They headed north, sorry to leave the bright lights but both of them had work the next day. A diner beckoned just across the George Washington Bridge, so they stopped for a snack.

Over scrambled eggs and toast, the women discussed the play from the opening to the standing ovation.

"When the show closes, Jack will move up in status and all because of you."

"Fate, Kathy, and kindness. When you open your heart, you never know."

Kathy giggled. "I have a date with Jack next week. How 'bout that!"

"I say way cool." And the friends headed for home.

A new life without Barry evolved. Activities to fill lonely hours were the most important. A flyer came from the Widow's Club to announce the local author, Charmaine Gordon, is booked to speak. Bring a note pad and pen. The topic is titled Everyone Has a Story.

The weeks had flown by and now another meeting. A thrill went through her. She recalled Kathy's words.

"Remember, it takes work to make new friends when you're all alone for the first time."

The evening of the meeting, Sharon applied make-up and put on a smile ready for another experience. Her blond hair had grown longer; she had a sparkle not seen in months. Satisfied with her appearance, off she drove to the New City Library for another adventure.

An older woman, radiant with experience, placed book after book on a long draped table. Slender hands caressed each title with care as she stacked what later she revealed as her babies. Not that she didn't have children but now they were grown and gone to all parts of the country, writing had taken their place. Standing back, the author admired her work.

Her lined face broke into a grin. "This is my favorite part, showing off."

The audience applauded with enthusiasm at her charm.

"Hi Everyone, I'm Charmaine Gordon, a widow just like you or maybe a bit different because when my husband died suddenly, I made up my mind to move forward, step by step, an outlet for loneliness, or even a real job. YIKES! And one day without training, I decided to write a story. I wrote and wrote, even learned how to use a computer, what a dinosaur I am, and finished a whole book."

The author lifted a book behind her. "My first book. A publisher offered a contract and I've been with her five and a half years."

"Tonight is all about you. I call this evening Everyone has a Story. Think for a minute or three. Recall a fond memory, funny or sad. For our purposes, go for funny. For instance, Grandmother brings a jello mold for dinner and decides to unmold it on the dining room table. She ends up wearing the mold dish on her wrist like a huge bracelet with the jello and fruit splattered all over your best lace cloth." She held up a hand. "True story. It happened years ago and we had a huge laugh over it every year. And now for the fun part of the evening.

You get fifteen minutes to write. Do. Not. Censor. Yourself. Have fun and write. When the bell pings, stop. Raise your hand if you'd like to read your story right now. Remember we're friends here. This is a club. Non-judgmental. Begin."

The guest author smiled to herself and for her own fun, wrote about the time her fiancé told her that making love has to be more than having chicken every night. She, the virgin, didn't get it. "You mean you'd like ham sometimes?" He cracked up and right there on Broadway, he lifted her over his shoulder fireman's carry and crossed the busy street at the red light.

Tears threatened to fall from the precious memory. Ping. The stop watch worked.

"Okay gang, who wants to be first?"

Kathy nudged Sharon. "You go."

And Sharon raised her hand. "Sharon Michaels here. I've never written anything but a business invoice or a letter but here goes."

She told the story about recently meeting the handsome stranger at the dog park and inviting him home for dinner. "I've always been a cautious woman, almost timid with my husband in the lead so as he followed my car, I figured I'd keep a kitchen knife in my pocket. Jack is a song and dance man in the revival of the musical Chicago and when he saw my piano, he asked me to practice for an audition. He's been offered, along with a few others, the part of Amos who sings Cellophane. I haven't played in years but it's like falling off a bike, you never forget. I ran my fingers over the keys a few times and we were into it. Jack got the part, sent me two tickets and Kathy came with me a few nights ago. It was amazing to think I helped him."

Major applause burst from the Widow's Club. Then Kathy read her amusing rendition of what she called Part 2 of the evening on Broadway with Sharon. Several other women read, loosened up by the first two. Others gave the gracious author their stories to take home and critique. She agreed to mail them in a week.

Before the evening ended the women had a chance to purchase the author's books and have them signed. As Charmaine packed up, Kathy took over.

"Ladies, we give thanks to our splendid author for giving us her time this evening. Let's have a round of applause and cheers for a terrific lesson on writing.

When Charmaine turned, she found the Widow's Club on their feet with a standing ovation. She gave an appropriate stage bow and left. Chris from the front desk wheeled the few extra books out the door to her car.

"Thanks, Chris. Did you have fun listening?"

"Some but I prefer thrillers and mayhem."

"To each his or her own." The author selected Sin of Omission, a book with murder, mayhem and love. After signing the book she handed it to the man who always helped her even when times were tough. "Good night, my friend."

# Chapter 11

After a tiring meeting with Fred and Corinne where Sharon questioned every invoice and expense they submitted, she drove toward home taking a new route. "Barry, they don't get it about working a nine-to-five job faithfully. It's like child's play for them and she wears inappropriate clothes to show off her boobs. Fred is such a dolt. He doesn't see men ogle his wife like they want to do more than have her measure their cabinets. Maybe I should close the company and call it a day."

At the red light she noticed a health club on the right. The sign said The Body Exchange. She pulled up, stopped and got out of the car. Women in bright tight leotards sat on bikes riding fast to nowhere, ear buds in place as they watched movies. Looked like fun to Sharon. Sweaty guys lifting weights were not for her. She pushed open the big glass door to hear music playing loud and clear.

A tall, muscular man stood behind the curved reception desk. He looked up and gave Sharon a smoky smile. "Well hello, stranger. Welcome to the Body Exchange. Join up with one body and leave with another."

"Nice opening. So you're talking about regular workouts changing your body."

"Yes. You appear to be very fit. I assume you're a jock of some sort."

"I played competitive tennis until my husband died almost a year ago. No more doubles since I'm single."

""How sad to lose the one you've loved, to begin again. And now you do what?"

"We have a company I keep going with mixed reviews. Tell me about this club please."

"Let's take a walk around." He called for a built with muscles young woman to take his place. "Sherri, hold all calls for me. Thanks."

He guided her through one room after another, each one with a different motif and then they arrived at the pool.

"Oh my goodness. A class with women exercising. How wonderful."

"Step into my parlor said the spider to the fly. By the way, my name is Chance. My parents felt they were taking a chance when they had me and so the name."

Chance escorted Sharon into his office after the chlorine scented pool area.

A Harvard Business Diploma on the wall. Very impressive, Sharon thought. There weren't any family pictures but there were many of Chance in competition mode, sailing and tennis to mention two.

He went right into sales mode to explain the various programs. At the finish line, Sharon still listening, his eyes gleamed bright.

"Oh hell. I'll give you a three month free trial to see if you like my club plus dinner with me tonight. Where do you live?"

Sharon had to laugh at his invitation and fast quips. "Nearby in New City. I am hungry. There's some wilted salad in the refrigerator."

He grinned. She noticed a very appealing cleft in his chin.

"So it's dinner then." He smacked strong hands on the desk as if to say case closed and rose from the leather chair. "Relax while I change clothes." And he disappeared behind closed doors to reappear soon after dressed in the club's white tee shirt stretched across his chest, Body Exchange in full view and what looked to Sharon like a very expensive black suit. She felt almost dowdy by comparison, still in her work clothes.

Under a darkening sky, Sharon left her parked car to enter the club owner's Jaguar.

"On the way back home from work, I passed your club. Intrigued by the sign, I stopped in. Funny, isn't it? Fate intervened. I meant to hang out with my dogs tonight, change into sweats, and take a walk."

"I love dogs."

He loves dogs, Barry. Am I acting like a foolish schoolgirl or what?

"Tell me more about you, Sharon."

"Oh, there's not much to tell. I'm not very interesting."

"Tell." His voice took on a professorial tone.

"Okay but promise to stop me if I bore you."

"Promises, promises. They fade to dust. Your voice is cultured. It soothes me." In one smooth turn of the wheel, Chance swung into a parking lot. Club X, the sign glittered in the dark.

"Is there a secret code in the name?"

Chance burst into laughter. "You're funny and delightful. There's an innocence about you unlike most women I meet at the club." He parked and hurried around to the passenger side to open the door for her.

"Thank you, sir. It's been a while since anyone opened a door for me."

"Shame on them, all of your gentlemen friends."

She shook her head at that. "Not many, Chance. How about none."

They entered into a world of dark and sparkling X's on the walls filled to capacity on a week night as far as Sharon could tell.

"So this is where the singles crowd hangs out during the week."

"I guess so. I don't have time for this." His hand gestured toward the long winding bar.

"Really?"

"Really. I'm a serious business man."

The maître d greeted him. "Mr. Chance, what a pleasure to see you this evening. Your usual table?"

A brief nod from the man she came in with and they were seated.

Another mistake, Barry. He lies, this man. What have I done going out with a stranger?

"A drink before dinner?" Chance touched her face. "Chardonnay, am I right?"

"You are and you? What's your preference?"

"You are an aphrodisiac to me."

"Oh my. Chance, you told me you had no time to come here and yet you have your own table. Explain because I'm confused."

She watched his hands polish the silver with a napkin as he sat silent. Then he lifted his head and half smiled. "Strictly business, my dear."

Uneasy with the change in him, Sharon changed the topic to food. "Is the steak good here? I so enjoy a juicy big filet mignon if you'd share it with me."

"I don't share filet."

"Oh. I'd like grilled salmon and I won't share crème brulee with you."

And so it went from flirtatious to odd, dinner with a stranger.

Three free months membership passed. They never spoke to each other again. One night at the club, one of the girls from the desk came over. "Chance is like that, kind of weird. Great business man and all of a sudden he turns cold. I think he really liked you."

## When Double Becomes Single

A year later, Sharon had finished with the Body Exchange. Her body looked just fine. Better than that, all the exercise and stretching improved her hip and now she felt strong again.

# Chapter 12

"Mom, you look great. Have you been working out?" Corrine sashayed over to compare muscles with Sharon. This was not quite a business meeting conversation yet Sharon laughed.

"At least it's not bad for an old broad. I did join a local club to fill my time. That and the Widow's Club and daily work keep me busy. Now let's talk business. How was your week?"

Fred puffed up to give the report. "We're doing very well. Corinne is a star salesperson, a closer on most every presentation." He handed Sharon, his mom and boss, a folder with invoices and expenses.

She shuffled through the papers before her. They needed a scrupulous scan before she was satisfied. Gazing up at the two of them, she had a need to speak once more, to remind them of what the business meant to her. "Always remember to be honest with me and Michaels and Company has a future. Trust means everything." Did she see them roll their eyes like bored children or was it her imagination? "Bring the kids around sometime. I'm their only grandmother, we need each other. How are they doing at the public high school?"

"Better than expected, Mom. Grades are high and they each made new friends so we're pleased. We'd like to buy a comfortable house to spread out before long. It's a buyer's market right now."

"You know Dad and I worked hard to build this house for you and Jeff. Life was different then but the work ethic remains the same. Sow and ye shall reap. Keep the sales going. There's a big market for cabinets and counter tops. You are a handsome couple. I'll give you some of my New York territory. It's too much to handle for one woman. Before you know it, you'll have your house."

They left after hugs and thanks for even more fertile sales ground.

Once again Sharon had the queasy feeling about her associates. They pushed like greedy children for more, a new house, a bigger car, more money. She'd given in for her own benefit. Too much work for one woman and she wanted to play the piano again. A shuffle of sheet music long stashed in the piano bench brought fond memories. With the newly tuned piano, she fumbled her way through 'Kiss Me Once, Kiss me Twice' again and again until the dogs crooned or howled along with her. Joy filled her heart as her fingers found a sense recall of where they belonged to make music. An hour went by and she didn't notice the passage of time. A roll of her shoulders and a new song found its way in front of her. 'I Love You for Sentimental Reasons'.

Magic happened that afternoon. A long forgotten talent returned. Sharon really played well enough to join the band. She called Kathy, her best pal.

"Girlfriend, I'm ready to join the Widow's Club band. After a couple of practice hours with oldies sheet music, all I need is an update on music."

"Will do. I knew you'd put your mind to it. I'll call Andrea. She'll fax a list and you start listening to current pop music. Oldies are good too for when you entertain elderly folks. Sharon, I knew you were up to the task. What a woman."

Two guitarists, Sharon remembered them from the first night, were on time at her home for the ramble. Andrea came right after. Eager faces greeted her when she opened the door.

"Hey, I'm Spike and she's Mike. We've played together for years, mostly in bars for fun and then our guys passed on. The kids are grown and here we are."

"I'm Sharon, pianist just catching up to a more modern beat. You can teach me. I catch on fast."

Sharon set out home baked cookies and wine on a tray in the living room.

"You're our kind of woman, Sharon." Mike sniffed the air and snatched a cookie. "Yum." She tuned her guitar and got into a rhythm to make Sharon want to swing her hips.

Andrea called them to order. "Our first gig is the home for the elderly in Pearl River not far from here. Take out some of the old sheet music you told me about. Let's get into that first. You made copies, didn't you?" Sharon nodded. "Cool. Sinatra is a good one to start with. Kids, are you familiar with Old Blue Eyes?"

"Sure. We're older than we look. You're the kid in the group."

"All Alone. Try this one." Andrea sang like a dream walking. Mike and Spike strummed and brought the song to life. Sharon did her best, an amateur with a heart.

"Damn fine, ladies, for the first time. Now let's give it a touch of jazz." And they did bringing a different life to the music. "Oh, man. Way cool. What do you think? Will the old folks enjoy the song?"

"I vote yes. The second way had more warmth and your voice struck me right in the heart."

"Okay, don't overdo it with the compliments. We have a long way to go."

They worked on oldies for an hour, stopped for cookies and wine to loosen up and get into rock and roll. Sharon ordered pizzas after three hours and the musicians stretched out to relax.

Andrea looked around at her new band. "We've got it goin' on right here right now."

"Ya think?" Spike shook her booty.

"Oh yeah. Next rehearsal is Sunday. Are we cool?"

They all echoed. "Cool." And just like that a band of no renown was born to do good works and bring joy to ones who need it. "Before we take off, Sharon you do understand a piano can't be carried around."

Sharon deflated like a punctured balloon. "So what can I do?

"Keyboard, girl. Carry case, plug it in and there you go. It even has a little stool to sit on. One thing, can you afford one? I know a guy..."

Sharon giggled. Spike and Mike cracked up. "Yeah, the guy found one that fell off a truck. Get me a good one and I can pay cash."

They high fived with a transaction in progress. "I'll call tomorrow with news and probably the goods."

Middle aged Sharon staggered her way upstairs forgetting the dogs and had to spin around to let them in. Her babies. As she washed up for bed, she talked to Barry. "Honey, you won't believe I've joined a band, relearned piano skills and had fun with three musicians. Four including me. It's a wonder and so much fun. Somehow I'm making a life without you, dearest. I didn't think it possible to survive and find it necessary to keep busy. What's more, it's good for me. I love you, sweetheart.

Rehearsals went well with everyone improving and then it was show time at the Pearl River Home. They wore bright red tee shirts with the logo SOMEDAY on the front the two kind ladies, Rooga and Naushin, made. They'd decided on the name because they were all in a state of someday, like Cinderella waiting for her prince to come. Black satin pants and boots. So much fun dressing for the show and anticipation hoping it would go well. Old folks were not known for sitting still. Maybe music would keep them in their seats. Maybe they'd sing. Lots of maybe's.

A crowd of people in chairs waited for them when the musicians arrived. Some were in wheelchairs, some in a kind of bed arrangement. Andrea encouraged the band to move in fast, set up and begin and have fun.

She smiled and waved at all the people. "Hi, I'm Andrea. Our band is called SOMEDAY. This is Mike and the one next to her is Spike and this lovely lady is Sharon. Here we go."

Away they went with the medley of Sinatra favorites and from the back of the audience a small woman in a robe began to sing along with them, her voice so pure and sweet. This encouraged more elders to join in and soon veined gnarled hands were clapping. At the end of the medley, the band applauded their audience.

"How about some Rock and Roll?" One of the elders croaked out his request.

"Sir, that's exactly what comes next." The hour proved to be a huge success. Even the nurses got into it dancing in the aisle, doing the twist.

They packed up as wheelchairs passed by with smiling folks waved. Kathy Chambers rushed up from the back, red hair flying, face aglow. "They loved you and want you back soon. What a hit!"

Grinning all around, equipment packed and Kathy with her sharp eyes called out. "Sharon, a keyboard. It has your name on it."

In harmony, the musicians said, "You can't carry a piano." More giggles and they were out the door.

Sharon said, "We're a hit."

Mike laughed, "In Pearl River, NY."

Spike jumped in with, "Next is Broadway."

Andrea sounded sad when she said, "Sure."


A gentleman walked over to Andrea as she threw her gear in the small car. "My name is Andrew Hornsby. I'm a talent agent. I'm here tonight to visit with my Dad and caught your act. My dear, your voice impressed me and I would like to represent you."

"This is a joke, right? I've been trying for years to get an agent."

"I'm legitimate. If you have time tomorrow, call me and come in. There's a new play being cast and I think you'd be perfect. Let me put it this way. Make time and come in. It's the chance of a lifetime."

Andrea watched him walk away and she ran to her friends. "Kids, something special just happened. An agent liked my voice and wants me in his office tomorrow. You've changed my luck. All of you."

A solid group hug and home they went to think about where oh where to find a singer.


Leave it to Kathy, the great organizer sent out a frantic call for singers in the Widow's Club. A fair amount of women showed up and right away auditions began with Sharon at the key board playing well known tunes from the fifties. The voices were okay, not strong enough, no belting out but sweet and some way off key.

A woman peeked in and waved during a breather. "I'm not a widow. I've worked at the library for thirty years and I can sing. Let me give it a try if you need a soloist." She signed the list. Marie McDermott.

Sharon grinned and shrugged. "Why not? We're pleased you stopped by, Marie. Is there any song you prefer?"

"Do you know Night and Day?"

"Oh yeah."

"Key of G might do it for me."

To say Marie knocked their socks off would be an understatement. Two of the other singers jumped in to flank her, whispered to each other. They sang in harmony, 'Pardon Me Boys, is this the Chattanooga Choo Choo', a favorite Andrew Sisters song that made everyone want to dance.

Kathy gave a thumbs up to Sharon. "Ladies, are we having fun or what? A new Motown, of sorts, in Rockland County."

Over coffee, the friends decided with some serious rehearsing, a three way program would be available soon, doing good for the community and each other. Eldercare homes, Developmental Disabilities shows, soup kitchens and possibly shows for returned war vets.

"Soup kitchens? Where did you come up with that?"

"That's why you met me and I met you, partner. We're do-gooders and about time."

A month later they had their first gig and soon they were booked for three months, one show a week.

# Chapter 13

As busy and full as Sharon's life had become, she missed something. On the way home from work the words 'do what you like to do' kept running through her mind. There must be tennis for singles somewhere. Without changing clothes, Sharon went straight to the papers. Book Clubs, parties, tennis singles. Yay! She called the listed number.

"The first session of eight begins tomorrow," the nice voice said.

"Where, what time?"

"Mahwah Tennis Center. Google for directions. A light dinner is included, all for thirty dollars. Credit Card, please."

"Oh my. Where's my wallet? Hang on."

She returned to rattle off the numbers to a stranger. He'd probably take a trip to Hawaii on her card. "Who are you? I'm such a dope giving you my card so freely."

"Ms. Michaels, I own Mahwah Tennis Center. My name is Jerry Marcus. I've been playing competitive tennis since I was a kid. This is a new eight clay court facility you'll love. My coaches are top notch. See you tomorrow and be prepared for a great time."

Possibilities. All you have to do is look around. Energy high, Sharon gathered her best pals for a love and a walk around the block. Tommy, on best behavior, marked every tree, gave a bark or two at other pets, like saying howdy and don't mess with us and soon, home looked pretty good to all of them. Some kibbles and water and they lay panting in their big beds.

Sharon had her nightly chat with Barry as she undressed. "It's almost summer, dearest. I signed up for singles tennis. God, how I hate the word single but that's what I am now. It's in Mahwah, not far. I'll use the GPS. I'm driving everywhere now and haven't had one accident because you taught me to concentrate. I hope I can play without you. Watch over me, Barry. Please."

A long red brick building, not twenty minutes from home, welcomed Sharon. A parade of men and women dressed in the latest tennis outfits entered the facility. She sniffed the air to tear up at the familiar scent of clay, the sound of a racquet whack at a ball was like music to Sharon's ears.

Eager to get out there, she hurried to the counter to sign up and find her court number.

"Jerry Marcus, please."

"I'm Jerry and you're Sharon Michaels, the well-known competitor."

He looked young enough to be her oldest son. "I expected you to be older, Jerry."

He grinned, dimples showing. "I do love older women. You say what you think. After you play, let's talk. You're on Court 4 with the best players."

Off she ran, bag in hand to find three men warming up. Their eyes widened to see the petite hot shot they'd heard so much about. She said to her slender partner, "Show no mercy. I may be small but I pack a wallop so go to the net and put the ball away."

They shook hands with the other men and warmed up nice and easy. It felt like coming home for Sharon, sliding across the clay like a dancer with the follow through high after a turn of the hips and lean in to smash the yellow ball.

They won the first set, shook hands and changed partners. A new shorter guy, serious, no joy in playing, loved to win. Easy set for Sharon and serious guy. The third set, she played with a young hunk who had lots of ink to decorate his arms. What a confident cutie. He called her Missy and told her he'd cover for her guaranteed.

"Thanks, hunk o'mine. Let's whip their pants off and eat. I'm hungry."

It was a battle, the kind Sharon enjoyed. The hunk slipped, fell on his butt and she saved the point by racing across the court and used a drop shot. They won by a snitch, had a good laugh and left the court to have a bite to eat, already paid for. A fruit cup and juice for Sharon. She knew not to eat too much.

The rest of the evening turned out to be a lot of fun with an exchange of phone numbers from a few interesting men and women. High from the tennis evening, Sharon couldn't wait to talk to Barry. She spilled about everything that happened. How she played, in great detail, just like the old days after a challenge and then about Jerry Marcus, so young and asked him what he thought about her going out with a guy so young. Hmm. No answer. And how come she accepted a date with him? Oh well. It's her decision. What a sweet young man, this Jerry. Time is moving along and she didn't meet anyone else to fill the gap. Maybe Saturday evening she'd have a bite to eat with him. Who knew what awaits? The pups, that's who. She laughed and ran into the house to be greeted by yips and kisses from two big babies who needed her. They are what matters in her life right now. No nutty guy from the Body Exchange; no young kid from a tennis club or are there possibilities? Of course there are, numbskull. There are always new adventures out there. Aren't there?

The big question in every single person's life is aren't there? Sharon showered and went to sleep in hope of a peaceful night.

Saturday night came fast and she met Jerry in front of the club where he paced. "Hey Sharon, I was afraid you wouldn't show and here you are."

"I'm true to my word, Jerry. Where are we heading, not far I hope."

"Nothing fancy but guaranteed delicious and close by. Hop in my car."

They were off and around the corner to Max's Deli. Swank, she thought but probably good.

Everyone greeted Jerry, obviously a favorite. "This woman is a great tennis player and she's signed up for singles tennis at my club, folks."

Sharon couldn't help but grin at the enthusiastic applause. They sat at a sparkling clean booth and were served fast. "The corned beef is sliced thin and lean, just the way I like it."

"Me, too. I like a little mound of potato salad on the side and a root beer."

"Me, too." An adorable waitress who tried to get Jerry's attention, to no avail, took the order. As soon as she left, they talked tennis and business until dinner was served.

He said the first week was beyond his expectations and felt a lot of it came from her signing up.

"That's not possible. Give yourself credit, Jerry. You're a figure in the world of tennis. Be sure to play tennis with your customers. By the way, I had the best time ever since my husband passed on. I thought I couldn't ever play again and there I was slamming the ball, hitting drop shots. What a fun time. So be sure you don't hide behind the desk. Mingle and play with your guests. They'll love it and you." She bit into the corned beef and moaned. ""You're so right. It's the best I've ever had."

After a fast hour, Jerry drove her back to her car. "Thanks for the good advice. See you next week. I'll let you know how business is going."

No foolish kiss this time. Sharon gave him some business wisdom and they had become friends.

# Chapter 14

Early the next morning the phone rang. Caller I.D. said Clarkstown North High School. What in the world? Sharon picked up. "Sharon Michaels here."

"Are you the grandmother of James and Lori Michaels?"

Her heart pounded with fear. "I am. Are they all right?"

"You are the designated caller, Mrs. Michaels. I'm Mrs. Van Buren, the principal. Their parents have left them alone while they are on a business trip to Florida. Did you know that?"

"No I did not. Are the children at school?"

"Yes. They are good students considering they're new here but I have a feeling life is difficult for them. Would you please come here so we may discuss this serious situation? I'm keeping this private for the moment."

"I can be in your office in half an hour. And thanks for calling."

A business trip to Florida. I bet and leaving two teens alone. Oh God. What next? And the kids are so near to me at that school. For some stupid reason they've kept them from their only grandparent. How selfish.

Sharon knew how to dress fast and she put herself together in a hurry. Half a mile away, she drove, mind in a whirl. Then she parked in the visitors section and caught her breath. Just like everything since Barry died, she'd find out what happened and in a methodical way all will be taken care. Sharon, don't kid yourself. This is a major problem.

All too well, she recalled where the principal's office was located but a guard stopped her to ask her name. He spoke into a walkie talkie thing and another guard escorted her down the hall. A light went on in her blond head. Protection for the kids and school. Rightly so in a changed world. She shivered with the thought of locked doors and the threat of possible terrorists in the beautiful United States.

"Thank you. You do an important job protecting the school."

His tight face loosened. He opened the door for her and there she stood, once again facing a Principal.

"What in the world happened with my grandchildren? Let me explain I hardly know them and yet I discover from your call they go to school so close to me. My son Fred and his wife never told me and yet I've asked them time and again to bring them over." Sharon sunk into the visitor's chair." Don't cry. Don't cry. So much for being strong.

A warm soft hand touched Sharon's. "Mrs. Michaels, James and Lori will be here soon and will give us a detailed description of what's been going on in their lives for what appears to be a long time. Please listen and be strong for them. They are remarkable youngsters. Between the four of us, we can find a solution to the problem. As mother's, that's what we do."

"You may not know I have a son Jeff. He lives in Denmark and is very successful in the dance world. His wife is a talented artist, also well-known and they have two little ones. Fred, on the other hand, married a disturbed woman. He has always been a problem child for us. I don't know why.

The first born with so much opportunity given to him. Now I've taken them into my business and at every turn, there's trouble. That's a bit of backstory."

A knock at the door and in walked two children. Sharon jumped up to embrace them. Lori looked so much like her. "There's no denying you're my granddaughter, Lori. We resemble each other. And James, handsome like your father but there's a lot of your uncle Jeff in you."

"I'm short." Lori's soft voice spoke.

"Petite like me." Sharon smiled although her heart broke in pieces. "Your grandfather said I was his pocket wife, petite but very strong. You both have an athletic look. Do you like sports?"

James face broke into a grin. "Oh yeah. Both of us are terrific in tennis, Lori is way good in gymnastics. You should see her on the balance bars. For an eleven and a half old girl, she's, well, just about perfect and can she dance. Wow!"

His little sister punched him in the arm. "Jimmers, I'm just okay, so far."

"Yeah right." He got right back into the conversation, so grown-up at fourteen. "I play the guitar and sax. We transferred from another school and haven't had a chance to fit in here yet and, and now this." His voice slowed with sadness.

The Principal sat aside as the family became acquainted. She watched the grandmother draw them out in a gentle sweet way.

"So what happened at home? You're safe here. I don't know if your parents ever told you how much I missed both of you and wanted to get to know you."

They shook their heads without saying a word. Damaged, Sharon thought but she'd fix that. By God, she'd fix that.

"Do you like dogs?"

"Oh yeah. We always wanted a dog but they said no."

"We took in two rescue dogs a few years ago and never regretted the decision"

Tears flowed from Lori's blue eyes. Her brother threw his arms around her for comfort.

"Please, grandmother. Please rescue us. We promise you'll never be sorry. James and I will make you proud."

With a swipe at teary eyes, James nodded his head.

The family made a circle of love and promise.

The Principal breathed a sigh of relief. All the technicalities were simple once she'd seen Sharon Michaels work her magic.

# Chapter 15

After school, Sharon met the children at the rental apartment. She waited for them outside, greeted them with arms wide open and the three walked up the steps into a dark hall. Four floors up, James opened the door.

"Home sweet home but not for long, right, Grams?"

"You bet. Take any clothes and sports equipment you own and let's get the heck out of here."

The kids scrambled around packing. Sharon read the note loving parents left for two children. "Kids we have to go on a business trip to Florida. Be back soon. Love ya. Money's the kitchen drawer." Bile rose in Sharon's throat as she opened almost empty drawers with plastic spoons and forks strewn around twenty dollars. Enough for what?

"We're ready." Their packs were pitifully empty except for tennis racquets and a few clothes. James had his sax wrapped in a towel and a guitar peeked out of his bag. Shopping was definitely in order but first, hungry kids needed to eat decent food.

Their eyes opened wide to see their Grams BMW. She opened the trunk, in went their meager belongings and they sat on the plush leather seats.

"Now what's your fave food and don't say pizza."

"What's pizza?" They all laughed. In spite of what they'd been through, Lori and James had a sense of humor.

"I so like chicken and potatoes and a little salad. The tennis coach always says to eat good food."

James grinned. "Sounds just about right for me. How 'bout you, Grams?"

"Perfect and I know just the place."

A secret smile came over her face as she drove home. She pulled into the garage. Barking was heard from the yard.

"Is this your house?"

"It sure is."

"It's so pretty and I hear dogs. Yippee!"

"So here's the plan 'cause we always like a plan, right kids?"

"Right!"

"Unpack your gear, take it upstairs and wash up. When you come downstairs, dinner will be on the table. After you meet the pups, we'll go shopping for a few things and then homework and bed. The bus comes at 8:30 a.m. sharp right here. Are we cool?"

"We cool, Grams."

"Let's go."

Like clockwork, the grandkids followed orders and soon the three of them sat at a table filled with just the right meal for hungry people. They helped clear the table after dinner and Sharon brought Gracie and Tommy in to meet them. Such wagging of tails she'd never seen before and the youngsters, cautiously at first, hugged and petted the rescue dogs that needed love as much as they did. On schedule, Sharon wanted the children to wear new clothes tomorrow so the dogs went outside, the kids washed and brushed teeth and off they drove to the Nanuet Mall where a fine shop had just opened for teens.

"What's the latest style for teens?" Sharon said to a young salesman but the kids had already wandered away, touching clothes and talking to each other.

He walked fast to catch up with the boy. "Let me help find something for you."

"Great. I like need jeans, a shirt, a sweater," he glanced toward Grams as if to ask if it's okay and she nodded. And the salesman went to work fast. Meanwhile, Sharon noticed toward the back of the shop, a section for girls. "Lori honey, come with me. We're going to have some fun." With the aid of a saleswoman, Lori tried on jeans just her size, two shirts and a sweater and they even had undies for her. They bought enough panties and a few small bras to keep her for a while. "Do you carry sneakers?"

"Yes. We have top of the line for every sport."

"Tennis is what we need."

"Sit over there and we'll get you fitted." A heavenly look came over the young, no longer neglected, Lori.

A worried James hurried over to his new Grams. "This stuff costs a bunch of dollars."

"I bet you need shoes, sneakers. They sell them over there where Lori is. Honey, I'm having a ball taking care of my grandkids. Enjoy it as much as I do. I bet you could use some briefs. We're starting a new life for all of us."

After an hour or more, they piled all the packages in the trunk and headed home. She had to sort out bedrooms while they showered and got ready for homework and bed.

"Thanks, Grams, for everything."

"And don't forget the chicken, Jamsey. I love my new pink bedroom."

"Mine is so cool, Grams."

"We'll need some computers for both of you but not tonight. You do use them, don't you?"

"We can teach you a few tricks. We started learning when we were really little."

She kissed them goodnight, cautioned them to finish homework and she'd see them in the morning.

Time to talk to Barry: "Honey, we have the best grandkids. Big trouble because our clever Fred and Corrine, the genius of the two, left the kids alone while they, the good parents, went to Florida on a phony business trip. I'm cutting them out of our business tomorrow and hiring a decent person to help me. I'm winding down after a crazy day but in a good way. I fixed up one guest room for Lori, she's almost twelve and the third bedroom is for James with a new bedspread, sheets and fresh pillows. At fourteen, he takes care of his sister. What a kid! More info tomorrow, my dearest love. It's wonderful to have youth in the house again. I miss you."

She called Kathy. Such an exciting event had to be shared with her best friend. "I'm sorry to call so late but you'll never guess what happened. The bad son Fred and his wife left my grandkids alone and now they live with me."

"Sharon, is this you? Wait a minute. Pour a little more wine for me, Jack. Thanks."

"You have company. You're drinking wine with a man. Wait a minute, wait just a darn minute. Jack from Broadway."

"You're so smart. So what's this about grandkids moving in? Isn't this going backwards? We are supposed to move forward with suitors and romance."

"Kath, I'm so thrilled to have my grandkids with me. Otherwise they'd be in foster care, shuffled around in the system. The Principal saw how I dealt with the kids and we had so much fun and well, good night. Say Hi to Jack. I think I'll have a glass of white before I go to bed." She ended the call, forgot about the wine and went to sleep with the alarm set for seven. Pancakes to be made for two hungry kids.

# Chapter 16

After waving good bye to her very own grandkids, Sharon thumbed through the want ads. One ad called out to her. Cliff Rankin, young, experienced in sales, computer savvy seeks position locally. She called and her heart gave a thump with the sound of a bright male voice.

Right away her future seemed brighter. The young guy, Cliff Rankin, turned out to be perfect. She checked his resume to find he'd graduated from Princeton, had a sick father and worked from home until his father passed on. Now Cliff was ready and willing to learn the business from Sharon.

She explained. "We began this business years ago with quality in mind. Top grade counter tops and kitchen cabinets at a time when homeowners could buy cheap from department stores. Michaels and Company got to be well known and we established a good reputation." She needed a deep breath to continue. "Barry, my husband, died suddenly, a few years ago. Here I am, not knowing enough to carry the company when my son, Fred, showed up. He wanted to help me work the company with his wife.

Needy at the time, I agreed and made a big mistake. They stole money from the checkbook, bought a big Ford SUV without asking and now they've left their two children, my precious grandkids, alone. I've taken custody of them so my life has changed in a good way. Have I bored you?"

"Not at all. Families can be wonderful and awful. As I listened I had a couple of ideas to protect your company."

Sharon settled back, relieved to feel she'd found a new partner. "Speak. I'll take notes."

"You need an office out of your home, and a new name for the company check. Let all of your valued customers know you and your new associate, that's me, are the only ones who represent Michaels Associates."

Together they made the plans, called a Realtor, got lucky to find a nearby office and went to the bank. With new checks under her name and the checkbook in a safe locked place, an alarm system was installed in the office along with CCTV. All of this was accomplished in one day. It is possible.

Sharon introduced Cliff to a few of her closest clients and made appointments for them to meet the next day. The rest had to be accomplished on the phone because the kids would be home soon. She called the school to find out about extra-curricular activities. The Principal chuckled as she looked at the schedule. "Tennis practice for both James and Lori. They'll be home on the after school bus about four thirty. I saw them today looking very spiffy, Mrs. Michaels." Sharon took another deep breath and relaxed.

Cliff had a way with the speaking to clients. Not pushy, just confidential and intimate. Before long their calendar filled for the month. At last it seemed that Michaels Associates was back on track and Sharon didn't have the burden of running a company all alone. Cliff stayed after she left for home. He wanted to perfect his conversation with the customers and make a few more calls. They shook hands at their good luck to meet and in one day accomplish so much.

The school bus arrived at the same time Sharon did. Kids from the neighborhood piled off the bus, and two of them were hers. Mine, she thought, so proud of Lori and James and realized they needed racquet bags and new racquets to fit their hands just right. She'd take them over to Jerry Marcus. He'd know what's what in that department and maybe arrange for coaches for the kids.

"Grams, how was your day?" James grinned when he hugged his new favorite person in the whole world. "We have the extra-curricular schedule so you won't worry about us."

Lori jumped into her Grams arms nearly knocking her over. "We had a great practice but the tennis coach said I need a different racquet."

"What a coincidence. I just thought the same thing. If you don't have something going on tomorrow, I know just the place to go."

"James, how come our Grams always knows just the right place to go?"

"'Cause she's our Grams. I'm hungry."

"Let's go, then." And into the house they went, dogs barking, the quiet house no longer still. Chocolate Chip cookies waited on the table made by Mia, the housekeeper, and cold milk in the fridge.

"Would you mind doing homework before dinner tonight? I've had a long day with business changes."

"You're in business, Grams? Like real work?"

"Oh yes, James. By the way, do you mind if I call you Jim or Jimmy? James is so formal."

"I never liked James. Maybe when I'm a hundred. Jimmy is cool. Can you tell the school?"

"Honey, I'm not sure but I'll try. Anyway back to business, your grandfather and I were in business for many years. That's how come we could afford this nice house. Today I hired a nice young man who will help me so I'll have more time for you and Lori."

"You're the best."

In the sweetest voice ever, Lori piped up. "I want to play with Tomlet before I do another thing."

"Tomlet?"

"That's her nickname for Tommy. Is it okay?"

"It's more than okay. So play with the poochies and always remember they are big and strong. Be careful. Pet them with long strokes down the back and talk to them. They are family. Wait, I'll show you how."

Sharon called to the dogs and they came running. She put her hand up and said "Stay" in a stern voice. The next command was "Sit." They sat, tails quivering. "Down." And down they went looking up at her for admiration. She stroked them the way she had explained to the kids. Slow and careful head to tail and in a soft voice she spoke their names.

"Jimmy, you're smart and strong. Give it a try."

He followed directions, one dog at a time. Gracie, the Labrador trained easy. Tommy, the younger pit bull took some work but Jimmy persevered and got the big husky dog to listen.

"Good job, Jimmy. They're getting to know you and obey is the clue. Now for Lori. Honey, you're petite like me so we'll go slow."

She giggled. "No prob, Grams. I've been watching and I paid attention so don't worry." Gracie was a snap. She followed Lori's soft commands as if she'd always known the young girl. Then came Tommy. He crept to Lori like a big baby and licked her hand and followed every command with a big sloppy smooch.

"I think Tommy's in love. Maybe it's her soft voice but she's his mistress, Grams."

"I agree. So every day keep up a training schedule with the dogs and we'll be one big happy family. Now wash and we'll have dinner."

And so began a routine where two youngsters joined Sharon Michaels home with very little adjustment. When she showed up at Mahwah Tennis Center with the kids on the weekend, Jerry Marcus took good care of them. New racquets, bags and coaches for talented young players. Or was Sharon planning far ahead without asking if the kids wanted competition?

She pulled them over for a family pow-wow. "I'm afraid I'm rushing both of you into the whirlwind of competitive tennis. Maybe it's because your grandfather and I were big at competing. We worked and played tennis. That's it. Oh and we raised two sons so we didn't start playing tennis until we were older. I don't want to force you into anything you don't want to do with your whole heart."

"We have a choice?" Lori bit her lip, her blue eyes looked around the club in wonder.

"You mean we can do nothing except homework and play with the pups or have a chance to learn how to play a great sport and compete?"

"Lori, what's your feeling about this? Grams is offering us a choice and she won't be angry, no matter what we say. Right?"

"Absolutely right, Jimmy. No pressure on either one of you. Perhaps you want to play and Lori says no way. It's okay with me."

Her grandchildren exploded with joy. "We both can't wait to learn how to play and win and we promise to do our best. Thanks for choices. We never had them before."

The words 'we never had choices before' rang in a proud grandmother's ears as she watched her grandkids take their first coached lesson.

# Chapter 17

"Mom, where are you?" Jeff's sweet face showed up on Skype. "I've been calling and calling."

"Hi, are you my Uncle Jeff?"

Jeff put his glasses on to peer more into the screen. "And who are you and what have you done with my mother?"

"I'm your nephew, Jimmy. Grams has custody of my little sister and me since our dear parents split for parts unknown."

"They left you? Oh my God." He shivered from across the world. "Leave it to Mom to make a good home for you both. How's it working out?"

"Lori and I have never been happier. Thanks for asking."

"You have to come visit, Jimmy. All of you. We have two little Danish cousins for you to meet. Is Mom around?"

"Oh, sure. Sorry I picked up but there you were and here I am. Grams." He called, his voice deepened every day, he noticed. "Uncle Jeff's on Skype."

"Thanks, Jimmers. Hi, my son. We've been so busy that somehow I forgot to clue you in to the latest."

"So I heard." He frowned. "That's a lot to take on now, Mom. Somehow I thought you'd maybe find a nice uh, man and make a new life."

"Jeff, honey, I'm thrilled to have youth in the house again. The kids are the best and then I play keyboard with a band called SOMEDAY, there's the Widow's Cub and my new associate is working out. He's a young guy named Cliff Rankin. Business is thriving now that the others ran away."

Jeff saw a change in his mother. Flushed cheeks brought a youthful glow to her.

"Don't work too hard, Mom. I will always take care of you and my niece and nephew." The call ended.

Inge's voice called out. "Was that Mamse?"

"Oh yes. And you won't believe what she's up to now." Jeff explained about the grandkids moving in. "Imagine at her age dealing with teens again?"

Inge smiled. "You have no idea what your momma is capable of. She survived the loss of her mate and step by step she's climbing back to build a life of her own. Most women would fall on their children, helpless. Not our Mamse."

"Inge, she even plays keyboard in a band."

With that, they both hugged each other, grateful to know his Mom was doing so well.

# Chapter 18

When Sharon's band SOMEDAY had a gig, often the kids would come watch them perform. They were a team. Fred and Corinne were never heard from again. One night at a performance for Developmental Disabilities children, Jimmy did a solo on his saxophone and to Sharon's surprise, Lori walked right up to the microphone, adjusted it with guitar in hand and joined the band. After the performance, she walked through the aisles and showed willing kids how to handle her guitar, a hand-me-down from her brother. The picture taken made the local paper. Tennis Star jumps in with a band to entertain at Camp Jawanio.

As Jimmy and Lori matured, Jerry Marcus would benefit from their wins in the USTA just like their Grandmother did. Sharon drove them to matches all over NY and NJ where they were gracious and sportsman like every time, developing good reputations. The world of tennis competition is fierce. Parents pressure their children. They buy the most extravagant clothes, travel all over and boast about their child. Sharon knew all about that world and avoided it. She kept it to a normal activity, taught her kids to be pleasant and ignore the brats no matter how well they played. Petite Lori smiled off court and was scary fierce when she hit the ball. Jimmy, long and lanky, covered the court fast; his opponents never had a chance.

And then her Jim got a full scholarship to Duke University.

## When Double Becomes Single

After many Skype calls over the years, Sharon decided on a family holiday to celebrate graduation and the many accomplishments of her grandchildren. She called Jeff. No Jeff. Again she called to no avail.

Where did the years go? One minute he's fourteen and suddenly at eighteen he's gone, or almost gone. And Lori just turned fourteen. And how about me? My journey began when I was fifty four and now I'm almost sixty. Barry, are you listening? Determined, Sharon made a plan for a trip. Time for a trip to somewhere wonderful before Jimmy got involved in the school schedule. Cliff, her faithful partner, would take charge of their growing and expanded business. Mia loved the dogs so that wasn't a concern. Just buy the tickets.

When the kids came home she said she had a plan. They laughed. "Here goes Grams with her plans."

"Works for me." Lori giggled.

"Let's take a trip to Denmark before Jim gets busy with college."

"Denmark?"

"We'll see the rest of the family there."

"Yes. I'm calling for tickets right now. We'll take a week."

Jim lifted his Grams and twirled her around. "Have I said you're the best lately?"

"Not today so this counts."

With tickets all set, she asked Mia to stay for the week and care for the dogs.

Mia, the long-time housekeeper, appeared to be thrilled to have the comfortable home to herself. "May I have wild parties while you're gone?"

A hearty laugh came from that remark until Sharon noticed Mia looked serious. "Um, my old friend, Mia, are you joking?"

"Actually no. My husband's such a stick in the mud, life is boring. Maybe a few friends would liven up this lovely house. We'd play cards, have a drink of two and, you know."

"All I know is I'm going and when I come back I want to find two healthy dogs, no blood stains and all my furniture intact. Have a ball."

Packed for the changeable weather, tickets ready to rock and roll, Skype did no good in locating neither Jeff nor Inge. With a lilt to her step, Sharon and the kids took a taxi to Kennedy International and off they went on her first adventure.

The huge airport appeared to be even larger than when Sharon traveled with Barry. Of course, he made all the arrangements and cared for her. The noise, the crowds all were a bit frightening. Going through the gate, she realized her trusty cane had been left in the cab, Yikes! Before the alarms went off because of total Hip replacement, she beckoned to an attendant. With great enthusiasm and white gloves the kind woman gave her a patting down and released Sharon.

This time she had strength on her side with two grandchildren watching every move she made. Passport and tickets in one pocket of her travel bag for the long first class flight. The on-time plane worked to their advantage. In her head, the words, "Forget your troubles and just be happy," went round and round. No thoughts of business worried her.

Sharon Michaels, you're on a journey. Fortunately, she'd studied Danish language and spoke it fairly well. The old tape was in good shape in her bag with ear buds to use during the trip.

"Ma'm, you have a twinkle in your eyes." The attractive young attendant who reached for her tickets smiled. "You might be up to mischief." Sharon fumbled through her bag and pulled out Kleenex. "Oh this is too silly. I'm excited to be traveling and this time I have my best companions with me." Then she found the tickets and passports. "There." She stumbled, realized her hip hurt and she'd lost her cane. He took her arm and escorted her to a fine comfortable seat. "Thanks. You're a sweetie."

"So are you, Ms. Michaels. I'll search the lost and found for another cane to keep you comfortable. Meanwhile, how about a drink to relax you before dinner?"

"You're too kind." Sharon flashed a smile, asked for Chardonnay and settled into the lush seat to refresh her Danish. Inge would be so pleased with her effort. Jimmy and Lori got a tour of the plane while she settled in.

A distinguished man in uniform sat two seats apart from Sharon. With thick gray hair, hazel green eyes, he cut quite a figure wearing a lot of medals on his chest. The Danish speaking tablet fell off her lap. Embarrassed, Sharon made an effort to reach it but he got there first.

"Lovely lady, allow me to help you." Examining the old Learn Danish Fast, he chuckled, his voice deep and warm. "So you're learning a foreign language. Well good for you. Danish is the most difficult one I've ever tried to conquer. Are you going to Denmark and may I ask what your name is?"

"Sharon Michaels. My son and his wife live there. He is Jeffery Michaels, School of the Dance with a Dance Theater."

"What a coincidence." His smile lit up the cabin. "I've had the pleasure of seeing a performance there a while back. Your son is impressive. He danced that night, so funny and charming. I'm Colonel Lawrence Roberts from Chicago, Illinois and all over the world." He eased a seat closer. "I'm headed to Berlin for a major conference. I bet anything we, you and I, can hook up in Copenhagen."

She giggled. "Yes, that is if my family is home. I made a silly mistake by calling, not finding them

home and just hopping on a plane with my grandchildren. Here they are. "Jimmy and Lori, meet Colonel Roberts." Lori gave her usual brilliant smile and with her soft voice said hello. Jim did the manly handshake. "By any chance do you know how to Skype from the plane?"

"Dear lady, right now my job is communications. Give me the number. I'll call right now." The colonel wrote Jeff's number and called. No one answered. "Where might they be?"

Puzzled, Sharon considered the possibilities. "The children are young. Perhaps they've gone to their summer house an hour away from Copenhagen but that would leave me sitting on a cold step outside their home. Not the best plan. Oh dear. What a mistake I've made. I'm just a dumb widow."

"Sharon, war is a terrible mistake. Consider this a positive adventure. Give me your name and number so I may rescue you."

They laughed at the odd situation two strangers found themselves in. The drinks came and they toasted to new friends.

"Actually my husband died a few years ago. Ever since then, I've been putting myself back together, to figure out who I am. And now I've decided I'm strong. Are you married?"

A look of pain crossed his face. "Not for a long time. She hated the military, packed up my daughters, and left."

A touch on his hand seemed a good gesture right then. "Lawrence, I'm sorry your life took such a bad turn."

"Deceased husband, foolish ex-wife. Life isn't perfect. As for me, right now I'd like a filet mignon with steamed vegetables and a Black Daniels. What's your pleasure, pretty woman?"

"Hmm. Broiled salmon with veggies and crème brulee and I don't share."

The colonel summoned the smiling attendant to place the orders for friends in such a short time.

Busy with the colonel, for the first time in years, Sharon allowed the kids to sit wherever they pleased without hovering. Growing up, no longer the frightened children of the past, they would order and enjoy their meals.

Little did she know, her grandkids were watching


"What's with this colonel guy? I think he likes our Grams."

"And why not, she's pretty like you are, little sister. Older folks are entitled to a love life, too."

"Where'd you learn that, big bro? Sex education 101?"

"Shh. She just shared her dessert with him. This looks serious. I'll have to talk to him. Find out what his intentions are."

"If she falls asleep on his shoulder, then it's time to make a move, Jimmy."

Like hawks they finished dinner, every morsel, and kept watchful eyes trained on the colonel and their dearest Grams.

"Okay, Lori, it's time for our move."

"Our move? I didn't know you wanted me to play back-up."

"The time is now." Jimmy grabbed her hand and they moved along the aisle to stop in front of the giant of a man with medals all over his jacket.

Jimmy cleared his throat. The colonel lifted his head up at him with a steely gaze. "Colonel, Sir. We met before. Our grandmother introduced us. My sister and I noticed you and Grams, in a very short time, have become uh..."

"Friendly." Lori piped up in her soft voice. "And we're concerned, well, we want to know what your intentions are because if this is a fling, we won't allow it." She peered up at her big brother. "Right, Jim?"

"Exactly right. We won't let anyone hurt our Grams. Uh, Sir."

Colonel Lawrence Roberts lowered his head and nodded. He hid a smile that threatened to shine. "Thank you for being so forthright. Sometimes you meet someone and you know she or he is the one. The minute I saw your beautiful grandmother, I knew I could never let her go and I do believe she feels the same way. There's a song about that kind of love. Maybe you've heard it. Some Enchanted Evening you will meet a stranger and once you have found her, never let her go."

Lori felt tears fall. Her brother wiped her eyes. "That's from South Pacific."

"I'm pleased you both had the guts to speak to me. She's done well with you. Now scat so I can enjoy the feeling of her sweet head on my shoulder because I'm deplaning in Germany. I have a conference in Berlin and then I'm coming back for a big talk with Sharon in Copenhagen."

After the kids returned to their seats and Sharon continued to doze, several times Lawrence Skyped her son's number again to no avail. The last resort was to contact a friend with connections who found out that Jeff Michaels had indeed gone to his summer house for a short vacation just as Sharon suspected. The colonel, who had fought in many battles over year in the military, wondered how the hell to fix the widow's situation. Due in Berlin for a week's conference as soon as he landed, curses ran through his mind until he slept, arms around the dozing woman who had captured his heart in just a few hours.

By the time the plane landed, he had a plan. He contacted another connection. "Fritz, this is urgent. I'll pay you back ASAP. Jeffrey Michaels, the well-known director of a major Dance Company in Copenhagen doesn't know his mother is coming for a visit from New York but the catch is, he's not home. Use your resources to find his summer house one hour from Copenhagen. Tell him to Skype her that she's on the way to visit from the states and he should be there. He doesn't want her and his niece and nephew to sit on a cold stoop waiting for her son and family. Got it? Okay. Call me back, man. You won't regret it."

Sharon blinked awake, fussed with her hair and peered at the tall man who still held her in his arms. "Where are we?"

"Not Denmark, my dear. You have a way to go. Not too far. I'm deplaning now to be at a meeting in Berlin. I have your numbers and if it's okay with you, I'll meet you in Copenhagen next week."

"You will?"

"Yes, I will if you are agreeable."

"Lawrence, I've had the time of my life with you in a few hours." She reached up to kiss his cheek. He beat her to the punch with a real sweet kiss where it belonged.

"I have a resource trying to find Jeff's phone number at his summer house."

"What? Oh God, I've caused a lot of trouble for you just because I rushed to get here." She cried big tears.

"Then we wouldn't have met." He kissed away her tears. "Listen to me. I'll find Jeff and he'll come home to his dearest Mom. One thing for sure, Sharon, I'm not letting you out of my life." He gathered his bags and left. Then he hurried back. "I have your son's phone number and address." One more kiss and he left.


The little family transferred planes and on to Denmark they flew. The sun shone, flowers bloomed along the way from the airport to Copenhagen. A weary Sharon gave the driver the address and relaxed with hopes that the family would be home when she arrived. She paid the driver, admired the spacious home and rang the bell. No one answered.

"Grams. Stop with the tears right now. We're here. Uncle Jeff is coming soon, I bet." The kids hoisted the bags up to the wide expanse of steps. Sharon huddled with Lori on the cold stone step surrounded with the luggage. A woman hurried up the street to greet them.

"Inge and Jeff's mamse and children? Welcome."

She handed each of them a warm cupcake fresh from the oven.

"Delicious." Sharon spoke in Danish best as she could. Another neighbor delivered a carafe of tea and soon a party gathered on the front stoop.

"Mamse!" Her family piled out of a Volkswagon.

"Darlings. I've spoiled your vacation. I'm so sorry."

"Mom, I don't know how you did it but we got calls from the Secret Service. You met a VIP on the plane to get so much attention."

"Yes, dear. He's a very nice man, a colonel in the Air Force. He's in Berlin at a conference and plans to be here to meet all of you in about a week. Now let me see my babies." With arms wide open, she called, "Emma, Hans, come to Grams. And these are your cousins, Jimmy and Lori." They ran to the new relatives from America with hugs and kisses. The family thanked the neighbors for the party and piled into the pretty house.

Jeff took the kids for a tour around the house. "I'm sorry you two had a scum bag life with your rotten parents but that's over. Your Grams is the best. You never know when you have kids. All parents can do is the best they know how. Here I am, a happy successful man with a talented wife and two kids. My parents were great with me and from what I've heard, Grams adores the two of you. You play tennis, huh?"

"Yes. We both do. I got a scholarship for college. That will make life easier for our Grams. Sister is heading in the same direction. We got very lucky with Grams opening her heart to us. We..." The tall strong young man had tears flowing. His little sister threw her arms around him and rubbed his back.

"Consider me a close friend and I am your uncle always."

After games, songs and ordered-in dinner, the children were off to bed under Sharon's strict eye.

Inge and Jeff wanted to hear every word about the business, the trip, and more, so they lounged by the fire and Sharon opened up.

"Kids, you're going to proud of your mom. I was in a total foolish mess ready to give the business away to keep peace. Slowly, step by step, I got stronger and used my brains. It took a while and every night I talked to Barry about what was going on. Now I have my grandkids and knew we had to fly away to you before Jimmy goes to college. Mia, my faithful housekeeper is having a wild time at home with parties and caring for the dogs. I actually hired a computer guy to run the business and rented a small office, got new checkbooks and invoices. My next door neighbor wanted more than I had to give so goodbye jerk and then I called, didn't find you home and just took off. That's the dumb part." Sharon caught her breath.

"Mom, you did all that without Dad taking care of you."

"I think Mamse is all grown up and what about this colonel?"

"Oh, very, so very nice. I even shared my crème brulee!"

"That's a very big deal for you, Mom."

They all laughed over this.

"Bedtime everyone."

Inge took charge. "We'll talk more in the morning. With you and the big kids here, Jeff and I can get a lot accomplished."

"This is my pleasure. We'll have so much fun."

The next few days were spent getting to know Emma and Hans. At five and six, they were full of mischief. A park was close by and neighbors came to visit. Jimmy and Lori prowled the streets and checked out the city.

They were in the playroom drawing one morning when a knock at the door sent the little ones flying. "Wait for me." Sharon called out a moment too late. Hans had already dragged the heavy door wide open.

Two small children gazed way up to see the impressive colonel in his Air Force Uniform studded with medals across his big chest. He swept them all in his arms.

"Who is the man?"

"Is he your boyfriend?"

Breathless, Sharon said, "You returned."

"I always keep my promises. Always."

*A love story never ends.*

# More Great Books by Charmaine Gordon

**ALSO IN AUDIOBOOK! OPTIONED FOR TELEVISION MOVIE!**

## *To Be Continued*

Elizabeth Malone wakes up the morning after an amazing night of passion with her husband of forty years to find a note: Dear Lizzie, it's not you, it's me. Abandoned by her husband, disappointed in daughter Susie's casual attitude Dad's having a mid-life crisis, Beth decides to re-establish herself as the winner she once was. When Frank Malone returns, he's in for a big surprise!

***River's Edge Trio, Volume 2*** by Charmaine Gordon
Three stories in the Charmaine Gordon series River's Edge, combined in one volume. Breaking New Ground, Bridging the Gap, and Spreading Her Wings. These Charmaine Gordon stories of love, passion, and suspense set in River's Edge, the small town with the big heart, are also available as singles in all ebook editions

***Breaking New Ground***
River's Edge comes together to protect Celia Brown's property when the CEO of a major construction company claims a part of her property... and he has no idea who he is messing with. The elderly widow and her six year old granddaughter prepare for battle. Romance, suspense, and more.

### Bridging the Gap

Anna Youngblood and James Chandler have problems. His little
daughter overheard his ex say she never wanted kids; Anna must make
amends for breaking rules of her tribe; he has a serious concussion... and
she's pregnant. Can this couple find happiness in River's Edge?

### Spreading Her Wings

Kindness to Strangers in River's Edge rubs off on all who live there.
Sally Kirkwood responds to an emergency call from a friend one early
morning. A daughter is missing and with Sally's skill as a reporter, she
finds her at an audition in NYC. Thus begins an adventure of show
business, unfaithfulness, forgiveness and success.

### River's Edge Trio,Volume 1

River's Edge where Kindness to Strangers is the Motto... Three stories of
small town Americana, where anything is possible. She Didn't Say No,

Housebroken, and Help Wanted. These Charmaine Gordon stories of love, passion, and suspense set in River's Edge, the small town with the big heart, are also available as singles in all ebook editions.

### *She Didn't Say No*
Grace didn't say no to the Big Man On Campus, Scott Dwyer. And then her life changed... Years later, a too-close encounter of an unpleasant kind with a skunk and Scott's German Shepherd reunites the former lovers. What happens in between are their stories of beginnings and endings and love lost, then found.

### *Housebroken*
Sally and Steve Atwood must make a big adjustment – a fair number of them, actually – when after thirty-five years, three grown children, and a lifetime of memories, they are alone, together, at last... And, then they found River's Edge, a small town with big heart, stories to tell that will warm your heart, make you smile, and turn a dreary day into a day of hope for the Kindness of Strangers.

### *Help Wanted*

Steve and Sally Atwood have some big adjustments to make when they move to River's Edge. Afraid he is losing Sally to a more exciting world, Steve panics, but despite Sally's lecherous new boss, together they rediscover all the love of their thirty-five years together and all the... excitement... that brings to their lives.

### *Farewell, Hello*

That first kiss... that first incredible, agonizing, bellyache-making first kiss. Soon, Joy and Danny are inseparable, planning a future – a life, together. A kiss goodbye couldn't prepare the highschool sweethearts for all that lay ahead. A family crisis, a tornado, and the Korean War brought their plans to a screeching halt, and changed their futures... but maybe not their forever.

### *The Beginning...Not the End, Volume 1*

The first three stories in the series of Mature Romance combined in one volume. Instant Grandpa, Book 1; Young at Heart, Book 2; and Before the Final Curtain, Book 3. These Charmaine Gordon stories of love, passion, and suspense starring sexy seniors are also available as singles in ebook.

### *Instant Grandpa*

Summer at the Jersey Shore just got hotter… Take one widower grandfather, add two little grandkids, and widowed grandmother with a small granddaughter. Mix well. Stir in sun drenched beach days and moonlit nights. What have you got? A kite flying high with a new tail; an author writing a book to sort out emotions; a talented boy with his mother returned to claim the prize.

### *Young at Heart*

Book 2 in the series The Beginning...Not the End. Seventy year old Joyce Campbell expected her new left hip to heal at Helen Hayes Rehabilitation. What she didn't expect was to fall in love with the distinguished silver haired Collin Brody who wouldn't give her a second glance. Until Kizzy, the therapy dog comes into Collin's life…and into his heart. What happens next? The Beginning, Not the End.

### Before the Final Curtain
Book 3 in the series The Beginning...Not the End. Once lovers, aging actors collide on stage as stars in a romantic comedy written and directed by a manipulative director. Add to the mix the talented assistant, a tough stage manager, one prominent costume designer, two young actors, secrets and gossip. Show business. There's no business like it.

### The Beginning...Not the End, Volume 2
Three more stories in the Charmaine Gordon series of Mature Romance combined in one volume. No Time for Green Bananas, Book 4; She Didn't Say No, Book 5; and Dr. D and the Dad, Book 6. These Charmaine Gordon stories of love, passion, and suspense starring sexy seniors are also available as singles in ebook.

### No Time for Green Bananas
Celeste Hamlin, seventy-five year old widow, has a goal... conquer the six mountains in the Saranac Lake region before deciding what to do with the rest of her life. Sixty-two year old Professor Paul Harris, meets the dynamic Celeste, and recalls the last words his wife said before she passed. "Find another love and begin again." Will they begin again?

## *She Didn't Say No*

Grace didn't say no to the Big Man On Campus, Scott Dwyer. And then her life changed... Years later, a too-close encounter of an unpleasant kind with a skunk and Scott's German Shepherd reunites the former lovers. What happens in between are their stories of beginnings and endings and love lost, then found.

## *Dr. D and the Dad*

A trip over a mound of sand on the beach begins a journey for Diane O'Rourke and Tony Flannigan. She's a pediatrician, a bit over weight; he has a foster care home with three children under his sheltering wing... and a dark secret. Can they overcome the past and make the future work for them? They might just find the initial trip was well worth it.

### The Catch

Tom Donnelly, once known as The Catch – every woman's dream guy, has fallen down every rung of the ladder he once worked so hard to climb. On New Year's Day, he realizes just how far he's fallen, and makes a list of resolutions to change his life. He vows to regain the trust lost from his family, his law firm, and his friends – and maybe even find the right woman this time.

### Sin of Omission

A twist of fate intervenes when Shelley keeps a secret that threatens to break apart the Costigans and her future. A mysterious client, Deanna Rose, enters Haven, victim of a savage beating under strange circumstances. Shelley investigate and finds Ms. Rose has an unsavory past. With the reputation and safety of Haven at stake, Shelley is at risk to lose everything and everyone she cares about.

### *Reconstructing Charlie*

Charlie Costigan has a secret. Home life gone from bad to the worst when she protects her mother from another vicious attack by her drunken father. Midnight. Clothes thrown into an old suitcase, she races for the bus with a letter to an unknown aunt and uncle. "This is my daughter. Embrace her as if she were your own." Determined, Charlie begins again. Alone with her secret.

### *Now What?*

I held his cooling hand and asked the two words spoken many times during our years together. "Now what?" This time there was no response. I was on my own for the first time. When my fingers touched his wedding ring, I slipped it off and held it in my fist. The gold band was warm. I clung to him. "Come back to me, dearest." Sometimes what you wish for is more than you can live with.

### *Starting Over*

Each morning, Emily Kendrick runs on the hard-packed sand of St. Augustine Beach to clear her mind and heal her heart. From the widow's walk of the house perched high on the dunes, a man trains his binoculars on Emily…

### *To Be Continued*

Elizabeth Malone wakes up the morning after an amazing night of passion with her husband of forty years to find a note: Dear Lizzie, it's not you, it's me. Abandoned by her husband, disappointed in daughter Susie's casual attitude Dad's having a mid-life crisis, Beth decides to re-establish herself as the winner she once was. When Frank Malone returns, he's in for a big surprise!

# Author Charmaine Gordon

**Charmaine Gordon** writes books about women who Survive and Thrive. Her motto is take one step and then another to leave your past behind and begin again. Six books and several short stories in three years, she's always at work on the next story. The books include *To Be Continued, Starting Over, Now What?, Reconstructing Charlie, Sin of Omission* and *The Catch*, and her series of Mature Romances, The Beginning...Not the End, including the stand alone novellas, *She Didn't Say No* and *Farewell, Hello.*

"I didn't realize at the time while working as an actor in NYC, I'd become a sponge soaking up dialogue, setting, and stage directions. I learned many tools of writing during the years watching directors like Mike Nichols and actors including Harrison Ford, Anthony Hopkins, and Billy Crystal. And would you believe, I was Geraldine Ferraro's stand-in leg model, my first job giving me entrée into all the Unions needed to work. When the sweet time ended, I began another career and creative juices flowed."

You can reach Charmaine at
http://AuthorCharmaineGordon.wordpress.com